MYTH-O-MANIA

VI

KEEP A LID ON IT, PANDORA!

BY
KATE McMULLAN

For Priya and Daniel Larson

STONE ARCH BOOKS
a capstone imprint

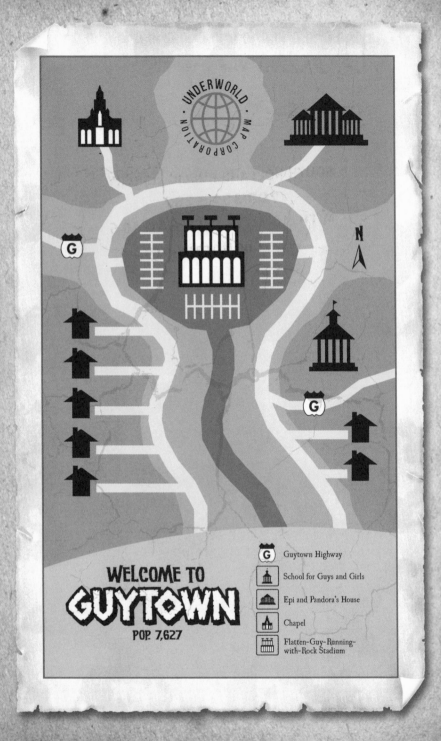

UNDERWORLD · MAP CORPORATION

N

G

G

WELCOME TO
GUYTOWN
POP. 7,627

G Guytown Highway

School for Guys and Girls

Epi and Pandora's House

Chapel

Flatten-Guy-Running-with-Rock Stadium

TABLE of CONTENTS

PROLOGUE

Guess who? Yep, it's Hades, back again to debunk another Greek myth. Want to guess why I'm debunking? The answer's a four-letter word that starts with the letter Z. If you guessed Zeus — bingo!

My *Underworld Dictionary* defines *bunk* as "claptrap" or "twaddle." (Check your own dictionary; I'll bet it says the same thing.) My little brother, Zeus, is the Boss of Bunk. He's so full of bunk, he ought to sleep in a bunk bed!

When Zeus decided to redo *The Big Fat Book of Greek Myths*, he bunked up the myths but good. He threw out parts he didn't like. He made up new bits and stuck them in wherever he felt like it. The big myth-o-maniac — (old Greek speak for "big fat liar") — basically lied up a storm to make himself look like a powerful thunder god. He heaped on the bunk so thick that now it's impossible for you mortals to tell what really happened and what he just felt like tossing in.

Take the myth about Pandora. You've heard the expression "opening up a Pandora's box"? The only reason anyone ever says that is because they've bought Zeus's version of the myth hook, line, and sinker. Here it is in black and white. Go on! Read it straight from *The Big Fat Book*:

THE FIRST MORTAL WOMAN WAS A MARBLE STATUE THAT WAS BROUGHT TO LIFE. ZEUS NAMED HER PANDORA. HE GAVE HER A BOX AND TOLD HER NOT TO OPEN IT, BUT SHE DID. OUT FLEW ALL SORTS OF EVILS — DISEASE, PAIN, GREED — THAT ARE STILL ON EARTH TODAY.

Total claptrap! Zeus gave Pandora a box, all right. A box full of really nasty items. But disease? Pain? Greed? No way. Those things were around long before Pandora showed up.

Zeus *did* give Pandora the gift of curiosity. That much is true. But the whole thing was just a setup so he could win a bet he'd made with me. The old bunk-meister tricked me, his trusting older brother, into betting him that Pandora would never open the box. Zeus put big money on her popping off the lid right away. But she didn't. It drove him so nuts that he spent years trying to trick her into opening it.

Oh, don't get me wrong. Pandy was curious. She never stopped asking questions. But she was smart, too. As curious as she was, she knew better than to open any nasty old box from Zeus.

Are you curious about Pandora? Do you wonder what it was like to be the one and only mortal woman in a world of mortal men? Do you want to hear the *real* story of Pandora and her famous box? If you answered, "Yes. *Yes*. YES!" then it's your lucky day. Just start on the next page. I've written it all down for you.

Chapter 1

WHO'S THAT?

We have to go back for this story. Way back to the start of everything. There was no Earth. There was no sky, no sun, no day, no night, no winter, no spring, and, for sure, no summer vacation. There was only Chaos, great swirling masses of matter. But inside that matter were the little sparks of all future life.

The first life to show up out of the Chaos was my granny, Mother Earth, otherwise known as Mama Gaia. Then came Night, Love, Day, and the Sea. Finally my grandpa, Uranus, also known as Sky Daddy, showed up. He went bonkers over Mama Gaia, and the two of them got married. Then those sparks of life really started flying. Together, Mama Gaia and Sky Daddy had bunches of giant children: the Cyclopes, the Hundred-Handed Ones, and the Titans.

Cronus was the youngest Titan, and Mama Gaia spoiled him rotten. In time, Cronus bullied his way to the top and took over the universe. He married the Titaness Rhea, and they became the parents of us gods. Rhea was a great mom — still is. But Cronus was not exactly a candidate for Father of the Year. For one thing, he swallowed his kids. No joke! Only Zeus escaped that fate. Finally, Mom came to our rescue. She fed Dad some herbs that made him urp us up.

After a time, we gods rebelled against Dad. That led to us fighting a huge battle with the Titans. It was an awful, destructive war. (And what war isn't?) Trees were pulled up by their roots. Hills were flattened like pancakes. Most of the mortals living on earth at the time were wiped out. Most of the creatures, too. But in the end, we gods beat the Titans. Then it was our turn to rule. That's when my little brother, you-know-who, lied, swindled and cheated his way into becoming Ruler of the Universe. I'm the oldest god. It really should be me sitting on that throne up on Mount Olympus. But hey, I'm not bitter about it. In fact, I prefer ruling the Underworld.

After the war, Cronus and some of his thug Titan buddies ended up doing time in the Underworld slammer. But not all Titans fought with Cronus. The ones who didn't were still around. Hyperion was the Titan in charge of all the light in the universe. When we gods took over, he was out of a job, so he made a major career switch and became a cattle rancher in the Underworld. The Titaness Metis stayed on earth. Zeus had a major crush on her. The Titan twins, Prometheus and Epimetheus, lived on earth, too. I guess you could say the story of Pandora starts with these two brothers.

Back then, I hadn't been ruler of the Underworld very long. I didn't have a TV. So I had no Earth Channel or HB-Olympus. I had no way of knowing what was going on in the realms above the Underworld except to go up and see for myself. Going to earth on a regular basis was out of the question. It was a nine-day trip! I couldn't astro-travel. (That's a little thing we gods can do when we want to go instantly from one place to another. We chant a spell and — *ZIP!* We're there. Sad to say, the Underworld is one of the very few places in the whole universe where astro-traveling doesn't work.) And this was back before I found out about a certain shortcut through a cave.

One day the Underworld sky was particularly gloomy. A crew of carpenter ghosts was working on my palace, Villa Pluto. They were hammering and sawing and drilling. Cerberus was only a little three-headed guard puppy back then, and the noise was driving him crazy. He was barking his heads off.

I had to get out of there. I clipped my Helmet of Darkness to my girdle — (old speak for "belt"). The helmet had been a gift from my Cyclopes uncles. When I put it on, *POOF!* I disappeared. I walked Cerbie out to the stables and asked a couple of groom ghosts to look after him. Then I backed one of my chariots out of the garage, hitched up my steeds, Harley and Davidson, and drove up to earth.

I got there nine days later. I took Harley and Davidson straight to the Asopus River to give them a drink. And there, on the riverbank, I spied two Titans, Prometheus and Epimetheus (better known as Epi). They were sitting beside the river. What were they doing? I couldn't quite see. But Prometheus was always doing something interesting. He could see into the future. And he was brainy. Even Athena, the goddess of wisdom, was impressed. I had to go check out what he was up to now, so after my steeds had drunk their fill, I steered them toward the Titans.

Epi heard me coming and looked up. He was the handsome brother, with his head of dark curls and his wide brown eyes. "Hades!" he called with a wave.

I stepped out of my chariot and walked over to the Titans. They were molding figures out of the riverbank clay.

"We haven't seen you since the kickstone battle ended, Hades," Epi said. "You know, the one where we Titans played against you gods to see who got to live up on Mount Olympus? The one that got so totally out of hand that it wiped out almost all the creatures and old mortals who lived on earth?"

"I remember," I told him. Did he think I could forget taking part in a battle that lasted for ten years? Besides, many of those mortals — called "Old Ones" — were ghosts now. They lived down in my kingdom. Epi was the sweetest guy in the world. But I wondered if he was all that bright.

Prometheus never even looked up. He stayed bent over, concentrating on his work.

"Look what Prometheus and I are making," said Epi. "Aren't they great?"

Dozens of half-finished clay figures were scattered around Epi. I'd never seen anything quite like them. "What are they?" I asked.

"Animals," said Epi. He patted one. "I think I'll call this a baboon." To my great surprise, the clay figure moved!

"Whoa!" I said. "How did you do that?"

"It's the clay here, " said Epi. "Still has lots

of sparks in it from the Chaos days." He turned back and studied the baboon. "I can't give you the gift of speed," he told it. "I already gave that to the cheetah. I can't give you the gift of swimming upstream. I gave that to the salmon. And the owl got the gift of smarts. Let me see what I can find." He put his hand into a big clay pot and drew out a small piece of parchment. "Oh, this is a good gift." He waved his free hand over the baboon and chanted, "I give you the gift of fast tree climbing!"

With that, the animal turned from a clay figure into a creature with bushy fur. It sprinted away. I caught a flash of its bright red rear end as it scampered up the nearest tree.

"Nice backside, huh?" said Epi. "I get a little far out and artistic sometimes. But I can't help it. I have to express myself." He smiled up at me sweetly. "Zeus told us to do this, Hades. After the big battle, he wanted Prometheus and me to make lots of new kinds of creatures to live on the earth. He gave us this big pot of gifts to give them, too. I can make a couple dozen creatures a day, no problem. But Prometheus is really slow. He's only done one!"

"Two," said Prometheus. He wasn't nearly as good-looking as his brother. But he was ten times smarter. He patted the figure he'd been working on. It began to move, but its color stayed the light brown of the clay.

I gasped when I saw what he had made. "It looks like you, Prometheus!" I exclaimed.

"It does, doesn't it?" the Titan said happily.

"It's a mini Prometheus," said Epi. "A Mini P!"

I spotted the second Mini P.

Prometheus beamed with pride at his new creations. "What gift shall we give them, Epi?" he asked.

"Hmm, let's see." Epi scratched his head. "He looks like he could use a super sense of smell. Oops! Wait. I gave that to the bloodhound already. Okay, what about the ability to jump a hundred times his own height?" He slapped his forehead. "What am I thinking? Gave that gift to the flea."

"Hurry up, Epi," said Prometheus. "They're

getting cold. Can you give them something to keep them warm?"

Epi frowned. "That might be tricky. I gave the wolf the gift of warm fur. The mink got the gift of soft fur. The raccoon got the gift of thick fur. The skunk got the gift of black-and-white-striped fur." He smiled. "There was a bonus gift on that piece of parchment. A second gift of this amazing scent gland. Stinks to high Mount Olympus!" He began picking pieces of parchment from the pot, looking at them, and tossing them back. After a while, he shrugged. "Sorry, Prometheus. But all the keeping-warm-with-fur gifts are gone."

"Epi!" said Prometheus. "You didn't think ahead. You've given all the good gifts to the creatures. Now there aren't any left for the mortals I'm making."

"Sorry, Prometheus," mumbled Epi. "You're right, as usual."

Just then I heard thundering hooves. Careening down the riverbank toward us at breakneck speed was a chariot decorated with glittering lightning bolts.

"Who's that?" asked Epi.

"Who would drive a chariot that gaudy?" I asked. "Nobody but the Ruler of the Universe, my conniving baby brother, Zeus."

Zeus! I thought about putting on my Helmet of Darkness and simply vanishing. But I was too late. The old myth-o-maniac had already spotted me.

CHAPTER II

WHAT SHOULD MORTALS LOOK LIKE?

"Whoa, horses!" Zeus yelled. He never could remember the names of his steeds. He pulled on the reins, leaving long skid marks on the riverbank.

Zeus jumped out of his chariot and hurried over to us. "Have you seen Hera?"

Hera is Zeus's wife. Queen of the gods. She knew Zeus was a shameless flirt when she married him. But she thought he'd change his ways after the wedding. Ha! Zeus is still a runaround. It makes Hera jealous. Now the two of them fight and bicker all the time.

"We haven't seen Hera," Epi told Zeus.

"She's out to get me." Zeus looked around nervously. "I told her that Metis and I are just friends now. But do you think Hera believes me? Not a chance. She is so suspicious!" He glanced over his shoulder. "If you see her coming, give me a heads-up, will you, Hades?"

"Relax, Zeus," I said. No way was I getting involved in one of his spats with Hera!

Now Zeus tuned in on the clay figures. "What are *those*?" he asked, pointing to the ones Prometheus had made.

"Mortals," said Prometheus. "You asked us to make new mortals to live on earth. Remember, Zeus?"

Zeus kept staring at the little mortals. "Why, they look just like you," he said. "Only shorter and squattier."

Prometheus smiled. "Thank you."

"It's not a compliment!" Zeus yelled.

The mortals ran and hid behind Prometheus. Zeus was scaring them.

"Don't make any more of them," said Zeus.

"Why not?" said Prometheus.

"Those pipsqueaks aren't what I have in mind for populating the earth," said Zeus. "I'll have my son, Hephaestus, make mortals. That way I can be sure they look right."

"These mortals look fine, Zeus," said Prometheus.

Zeus wrinkled his nose. "Not really," he said.

"What should mortals look like?" Prometheus asked.

"They should be handsome," said Zeus. "They should look like *me*."

Big surprise! The old myth-o-maniac is also an ego-maniac. I'd pity any mortals modeled on him. They'd be potbellied and balding. Zeus is always tearing around the universe. Always in a rush. He never remembers to drink his daily glass of nectar. Or snack on an ambrosia bar. So he hasn't stayed young and good-looking like the rest of us gods.

"Oh, come on, Zeus," said Prometheus. "I fought on your side in the big battle between the Titans and the gods, didn't I?"

"Of course you did," said Zeus. "But only because you looked into the future and saw that my side was going to win."

"True," said Prometheus. "But you couldn't have won without me."

"So?" said Zeus.

"So I want to make some more mortals like this one," said Prometheus.

"Oh, all right," said Zeus. "But not too many!"

"I won't make too many," Prometheus said. "I promise."

Zeus nodded. He knew that Prometheus was a Titan who kept his word.

"Hey, I found one!" Epi said. He held up a slip of parchment from the pot. "This gift will keep the mortals warm."

"What is it?" said Prometheus eagerly.

"The gift of fire!" said Epi.

"Oh, no you don't," snapped Zeus. He snatched the parchment out of Epi's hand. "How did this get into the pot? It's a mistake. Fire is for the gods. Only for the gods." He crumpled up the parchment and stuck it into his pocket.

"But these mortals are so helpless!" said Prometheus. "They need some way to keep warm. Earth gets cold at night."

"Fire stays up on Mount Olympus!" roared Zeus. "End of discussion!"

"All right," said Epi. "No fire for these mortals." He pulled another slip from the pot. "How about this?" he said. "The gift of making up games."

"Games," said Zeus. "Fine."

Epi waved his hand over the little mortals. "I give you the gift of making up games!" he said. And then he added, "Especially contact sports!"

Immediately the two little mortals faced off, joined hands and started thumb wrestling.

Hoofbeats sounded again.

"Ye gods!" Zeus exclaimed. "Here she comes!"

Hera's chariot was bearing down on us. The Ruler of the Universe ran and jumped back into his own chariot.

"Giddyup!" he cried to his steeds. Then he thundered off, with Hera hot on his wheels.

Prometheus frowned. He turned to Epi. "I just had a little future flash," he said. "It wasn't that clear. Something about Zeus giving you a gift."

"What was it?" asked Epi eagerly.

"I didn't see," said Prometheus. "But you know how sneaky Zeus is. Promise me you won't ever accept a gift from him."

"All right," said Epi. "I promise."

"Good." Prometheus turned back to his little mortals. He patted each one gently on the head. "All the animals have names," he said thoughtfully. "The old mortals are called 'Old Ones.' These mortals need a name of their own. I think I'll call them . . . guys."

CHAPTER III
WHAT GOING HAPPEN?

I stayed down in my kingdom for a long time after that. The carpenter ghosts had finished the addition to Villa Pluto. The Furies — Tisi, Meg, and Alec — moved in. These three ladies have huge black wings and snakes instead of hair. Each night they flew up to earth to punish the wicked. So they always came home with plenty of juicy stories. After the ghost workers left, Cerbie started barking at the Furies. Still, it was a fine time to be in the Underworld.

One evening I was in my den, sitting in my La-Z-God recliner. I had it flat out in "total recline." I was reading *Dog Training Made Easy* and had just gotten to the chapter on barking when there was a knock at the den door.

Cerbie leaped up. "Woof! Woof! Woof! Woof! Woof! Woof!"

"Cerbie, stop it!" He didn't, so I grabbed him by the collar. "Come in!" I called.

Hypnos, my first lieutenant, opened the door. When he saw Cerbie snarling with all three heads and straining to get at him, he closed it part way.

"Sorry to bother you, Lord Hades," Hypnos said through the crack.

"What is it, Hypnos?"

"We have a situation," Hypnos said. "Too many new ghosts are arriving. Motel Styx is bursting at the seams."

Motel Styx is where newly arrived ghosts go when they first get to the Underworld.

"But how can that be?" I asked Hypnos. "There aren't that many Old Ones left on earth. So how could there be so many ghosts?"

"I'm not good at figuring things out, Lord Hades," said Hypnos, putting a hand to his mouth to cover a yawn. He's the official god of sleep, and he's always wanting to doze off. "I'm only telling you what the desk clerk at Motel Styx told me."

"Right," I said. "Come on, Cerbie. I guess we'd better go and take a look."

It was a good thing we did. It wasn't the ghosts of Old Ones who were clogging the system. It was guy ghosts. Hundreds of them! Lost ghosts were roaming the Motel Styx hallways. They were moaning and groaning and complaining. The vending machines were completely emptied out. The bathroom had a line a dekamile long outside it. What was going on?

I jumped into my chariot and headed for the River Styx. When I got there, Charon, the river-taxi driver, had just brought over another boatload of ghosts.

"Charon!" I called. "What's happening? Where are all these ghosts coming from?"

"Earth, Lord Hades," said Charon. "Earth."

Charon is not exactly a merry-sunshine kind of immortal. I've never heard him laugh. But that day he was almost smiling. And I knew why. Ghosts have to pay one gold coin to be ferried over to my kingdom. The old miser was making a fortune. I wasn't going to get any more information out of him.

"Looks like I have to go up to earth, Cerbie," I told my pooch. "You want to come?"

Cerbie wagged his stump of a tail. Maybe he had a little barking problem, but what a pal.

I hurried back to Villa Pluto to stock up on fodder for my steeds, Cheese Yummies for Cerberus, and enough Necta-Colas and bags of Ambro-Chips to last me the nine-day trip. Then I jumped into my chariot and started up the Underworld Highway, a steep, rocky road that is the only way into or out of the Underworld.

Nine days later, my chariot rolled onto the edge of a forest on earth.

I reined in my steeds, and my eyes widened in disbelief. The place was *crawling* with guys. Prometheus's guys. They were sitting in the mouths of caves or walking on dirt paths between caves. With my own godly ears I'd heard Prometheus promise Zeus wouldn't make

too many guys. But he had. Way too many!
Anyway, this explained the population explosion
down in my kingdom.

The guys had grown since I'd seen them last.
They didn't look all that much like Prometheus
anymore. They had shaggy hair. And bushy
beards. They were wrapped up in layers of what
looked like tree bark and leaves. They wore bark
on their feet, too. And they gave off a very strong
odor.

A big bunch of smelly guys hurried over to my
chariot. They surrounded it, muttering things like
"Hubcaps good," and kicking my wheels. They
fired questions at me.

"What best time for zero to LX?" asked one
guy.

"How chariot handle curves?" asked another
guy.

"Can go off road?" asked a third.

Cerbie went into a low-level triple growl.

Suddenly I heard someone call, "Hey-hey,
Hades!"

Only one god greets me like that — my

wild-and-crazy brother, Poseidon, Ruler of the Seas.

"Hey, Po!" I cried, happy to see him. He drew his earth chariot up alongside mine. (His main mode of transportation at the time was sea chariot, drawn by a team of giant seahorses. But on land, he drove a sporty little two-seater.)

Now the guys ran to him. They started oohing and aahing over his chariot.

"Hey, party guys!" Po greeted them. Clearly, the guys were no strangers to Po. "What's happening?"

"Big Flatten-Guy-Running-With-Rock game today," said one of the guys.

"Gonna be great," said another guy. "Saber Tooths against Woolly Mammoths."

"Go Mammoths!" yelled a few of the guys.

"All right!" said Po, sounding very much like a guy himself. "And what's the scene after the game?"

"Big tailgate party," one of the guys told him. "In parking lot."

"We got keg!" said another guy.

"And plenty snacks!" said another.

"Right!" said still another. "Seeds! Nuts! Berries!"

Seeds? Nuts? Berries? Squirrel food! Even the guys didn't seem that excited.

Po turned to me and rolled his eyes. "You know Zeus was majorly ticked off when he discovered that Prometheus had made so many guys."

"I'll bet," I said.

"So he made a decree," said Po. "No hunting. All the guys have to eat are what they can pick off bushes." He shrugged. "Prometheus keeps begging Zeus to let them have a little meat now and then, but you know how stubborn our little bro can be."

"Tell me about it," I said. I felt sorry for the guys.

"Hey!" called a guy. "We go back my cave until game start. We make paintings of favorite players on wall of cave."

"And we look at them!" yelled another.

"Yay!" called yet another. "Pre-game show!"

"Go, Mammoths!" yelled one of the guys. And they all started to run off.

At that moment, a guy ran by shouting, "Hey, guys? Run to foot of Mount Olympus. Fast! Our friend Prometheus says so!"

"What going happen?" called another guy.

"Something!" the messenger guy shouted. "Something big!"

CHAPTER IV
FREE SNACKS?

"Come on!" yelled the messenger guy. "Follow me!"

"But game today!" another guy called to him.

"Can't miss game!" shouted another.

"This better than game," said the messenger guy. He turned toward Po and me. "Gods coming, too. All gods. Prometheus say so. Come on! Free snacks!"

"Free snacks?" cried all the guys.

And they ran off after the messenger guy.

"What do you think that's about?" I asked Po.

"Got me, bro," said Po. "But, hey, free snacks. Let's go."

The two of us drove our chariots to the foot of Mount Olympus.

By the time we arrived, a huge crowd of guys had gathered. A rope barrier kept them away from the actual base of the mountain. But Po and I drove our chariots around it. There didn't seem to be a gods' parking lot. Then I realized — all the other gods would have gotten here by astro-traveling.

Po and I pulled our chariots over next to Prometheus's wagon. I gave Harley and Davidson a couple of carrots. I gave Cerbie some Cheese Yummies.

"All right, guard dog," I told him. "Guard."

Po and I walked toward the other gods. I saw Hera, Demeter, and Hestia. I spotted Zeus. And our mom, Rhea. Tons of Zeus's kids were there. Plus a few Titans. Prometheus and Epi were clapping, trying to quiet everybody down. When he saw me, Prometheus gave a nod.

"Silence!" Epi called. "Okay! Now let's get started."

Gods are hard to quiet down. They all think what they have to say is incredibly important. But at last they stopped chattering.

"Thank you for coming today," said Prometheus. He stood between two tables. A huge silvery dome sat on top of each one. Very mysterious. "As everyone knows, Zeus, King of the Universe, has decreed that for the guys, there's no hunting."

"Bad decree!" muttered some of the guys.

I figured Prometheus was trying to butter Zeus up, with that King-of-the-Universe bit. But why? What was he up to?

"I've asked you Olympians to come here today to show you how it could be a good thing for all of us if the guys went hunting," Prometheus went on.

"What about the free snacks?" called Zeus.

"Coming right up," said Prometheus.

Epi began circulating among us gods with a silvery platter. It held roasted meat chunks on toothpicks.

"Wild boar bits," Epi told me.

I took one. Excellent!

After the gods were served, Epi gave snacks to the guys. They tossed them into their mouths and swallowed them down, toothpick and all.

"How are the snacks?" called Prometheus.

"Snacks good!" the guys yelled back.

"I want seconds!" yelled Zeus.

Prometheus smiled. "You could eat like this all the time, Zeus," he said. "Because if you let the guys hunt, they could give you part of their meat each day."

Zeus grabbed a handful of boar bits as Epi passed by. "Go on," he said, chewing loudly. "I'm listening."

"If you're interested in this deal," said Prometheus, "one of you gods can choose which parts of the boar or ox or whatever you get and which part the guys get."

"Let Hades choose!" cried Po.

"Yes!" called Hera. "He's the oldest."

It made me feel great to be nominated. But I knew I didn't stand a chance.

"I don't think so!" Zeus boomed out. "King of the Universe chooses. End of discussion!"

The other gods muttered. But there was nothing they could do. Zeus ruled.

"All right, Zeus," said Prometheus. "You choose for all the gods. You can pick this . . ."

He lifted up one silvery dome. Under it was a platter holding what looked like a big pile of juicy steaks.

"Yum!" cried the guys.

Now Prometheus lifted the second silvery dome.

"Yuck!" cried the guys.

"Yuck!" cried quite a few of the gods, too.

For on that platter was what looked like pieces of boar skin with slimy raw innards piled high on top.

"All right, Zeus," said Prometheus. "Pick your meat!"

CHAPTER V
WHERE IS PANDORA?

I'm glad you asked that. After all, this book is called *Keep a Lid on It, Pandora!* So you were probably expecting her to show up right away. Like on the first page. Or at least in the first chapter. But Pandora doesn't make her grand entrance until chapter VII. No, make that chapter VIII. So here's my advice: Keep a lid on it!

Now, on with the story.

"Whichever platter you choose," Prometheus told Zeus, "this will be the gods' share of the meat from now until the end of time. Go ahead, Zeus. Pick."

"Duh!" said Zeus, looking from the pile of steaks to the pile of sloppy innards. "That's a no-brainer! I pick —"

"Hold it, Zeus!" Hera said, cutting him off.

"Huh?" said Zeus. "What now?"

"Maybe we should all talk about it," said Hera. "Make the decision together."

"Right," said Aphrodite. "The steak looks a little thin to me."

"Things are not always as they seem," added Demeter. She sounded as mystical as the oracle at Delphi.

"Really," said Po. "Come on, Zeus. At least go up to the tables. Poke around a little bit."

"Sorry," said Epi. "No poking allowed."

"I never poke anyway," said Zeus. "I choose that sacrifice!" He pointed to the platter of steak.

"So it shall be forever!" said Prometheus.

"You keep saying that," said Zeus. "Are we finished here? 'Cause I am. I'm going to take this steak back up to my cooking nymphs. Have them throw it on the barbie." Zeus strode up to the table and grabbed the platter holding the steak. He whisked it away so fast that the steak slipped off the platter. We all saw that Aphrodite had been right. The steak was thin. Very thin! And hidden under it were not thicker steaks — but a big pile of boar bones covered with a thick layer of fat!

"What's this?" thundered Zeus. He picked up the little steak. He held it between his thumb and forefinger. It was thin as parchment. And riddled with gristle. "You call this a steak?"

"I didn't call it anything," said Prometheus. "You picked it."

"I *told* you to wait, Zeus!" wailed Hera. "Why do you never listen to me?"

Zeus stared at that skinny steak, horrified. Then he glanced back at the pile of fat-smeared bones. Finally, his beady eyes found their way to Prometheus.

"You have dared to trick the gods!" growled Zeus.

"Not the gods, Zeus," said Prometheus. "Just you."

"Not too smart, Dad," said Athena. "You should have asked me!"

"Bad move, Zeus," said Po.

"Oh, too much meat isn't good for us

anyway," said Demeter. "Whole grains. That's the ticket. And lots of fresh fruits, nuts, veg —"

"Stop yapping, Demeter!" shouted Zeus. "It makes my head hurt."

You'd think Zeus might have been grateful that at least one of the Olympians was sticking up for him. But he's never grateful.

"This was no mistake," Zeus said at last. He looked very sly. "Why, there's nothing I love better than a nice, fat-coated bone. Chewing on bones is good for the teeth. Does wonders for the gums. Thanks, Prometheus. I love bones! Yum!" He picked one up and started gnawing on it. He reminded me of Cerbie.

"Oh, for Mount Olympus's sakes, Zeus!" said our mom, Rhea. "This is more than I can take." She began chanting the astro-traveling spell. Most of the Olympians joined in the chanting. *ZIP!* They were gone.

"What we get, Prometheus?" yelled one of the guys. "Innards?"

"Right," said Prometheus, walking over to the table that held the gloppy intestines, stomach, and so forth. "You get innards."

"Rats," said several guys.

They all looked pretty disappointed.

"We still got berries," said one.

"And nuts," said another.

Now Prometheus brushed the innards off the platter. Underneath them was a big, thick, juicy boar steak.

"All riiiight!" roared the guys. "We got steak! We got steak!" They rushed over to Prometheus and picked him up on their shoulders. The Titan was titanic, so it took almost every single guy to do it. They paraded him around the base of Mount Olympus.

Zeus's chin was slick with grease from gnawing on that bone. He wiped it with the sleeve of his robe and shot a look my way. "You, Hades. You're big buddies with Prometheus. You probably helped him cook up this trick. Didn't you?"

"I have a kingdom to run, Zeus," I told him. "I don't have time for tricks."

"Humph." Zeus grunted. "Well, Prometheus is going to be sorry he pulled this little stunt. And when I say sorry, I mean *sorry*."

"Oh, don't be vengeful, Zeus," I said. "Those poor guys, eating berries day after day. It was pitiful. If you want a steak so much, have your nymphs come down to earth and get an ox."

"Don't tell me what to do!" Zeus shouted. "I'm king of the gods! I know what to do!" With that, he tried chanting the astro-traveling spell. But he was so angry and sputtering that he couldn't spit it out. He stomped off.

I walked with Po over to our chariots. My fearless guard dog was snoozing in the backseat.

Po and I said goodbye. He jumped into his chariot and took off. I was about to step into the driver's seat and take off, too, when the guys put Prometheus down. I waited to see what would happen.

Several guys ran over to the platter and grabbed the boar steak. They all wanted the meat. It turned into a big tug-of-war.

"Knock it off, guys!" said Epi. "We've got a whole cooler full of steaks in our wagon! There's plenty for everyone."

"Yay!" yelled all the guys. They ran over to the wagon.

Prometheus and Epi hurried over, too. Epi opened the cooler. He and Prometheus started handing out steaks.

They offered me one, but I said no thanks. I started to climb into my chariot for a second time when suddenly Zeus ran over. He shook his fist at Prometheus.

"I'll punish you, Titan," he said. "Look into the future, and see how you will suffer!"

"I can't see my own future very often, Zeus," said Prometheus. "Sorry."

"Well, if you could, you wouldn't like it," said Zeus. "And listen here. Maybe you fixed it so those mortals you made got the good meat. But —" his eyes lit up like live coals — "they don't have fire! No, and they never will! Never! So from now until the end of time, they'll have to eat raw meat!" Zeus started laughing like crazy. Still laughing, he managed to get the astro-traveling chant right. *ZIP!* He was out of there.

"Raw?" said one of the guys. They all started grumbling.

"Hey, simmer down," said Epi. "Real guys love raw meat."

"Anyway," added Prometheus, "pretty soon I'm going to bring you guys fire."

Fire! I almost tripped over my reins when I heard that. Prometheus had made Zeus sizzling mad already. Was he trying to get himself zapped with a thunderbolt?

"Yeah," Prometheus was saying, "and when you have fire, I'll teach you guys how to cook your meat this really cool way. It's called . . . *grilling*."

CHAPTER VI

WHAT NOW?

I waited until Prometheus and Epi had passed out all the steaks. The guys grabbed them eagerly. Then they ran back to their caves to eat them.

When the steaks were all gone, the Titans started packing up their wagon. Prometheus was whistling. He was very pleased about the way his little scheme had worked. I went over to him.

"Prometheus, I couldn't help overhearing what you said to the guys," I said. "About bringing them fire."

"The steaks were Part I of my plan," Prometheus said. "Part II is fire."

"Listen, I know the guys need fire," I told him. "And in time, if you play your cards right,

Zeus will give in. He hardly ever remembers his decrees. But he can hold a grudge like a pitbull. Don't make him any angrier at you then he already is."

Not that I wasn't completely on Prometheus's side. I was! But I didn't want him plotting against my little brother Z. That could be hazardous to his health.

"By the way, Prometheus," I added, "didn't you promise Zeus you wouldn't make too many guys?"

Prometheus nodded. "Zeus may think there are too many guys on earth. But I don't.

I got what he was saying. "Too many" was a matter of opinion.

"We think the earth could use more guys," Epi put in. "Lots more!"

"But I won't make any more," said Prometheus. "Not until I bring fire to the guys who are already here."

"Be careful, Prometheus," I warned. "You saw how nuts Zeus went when Epi brought this up before. He said fire for the guys was a big no-no."

"I don't care what Zeus says!" Prometheus shouted.

"Easy, big fella!" I said.

But Prometheus was really worked up. "I'm a Titan!" he cried. "I've been kicking around the universe for a long time. A lot longer than you gods. I'm a peaceful Titan. But if I have to tangle with a thunder god, I'll come out on top."

I calmed Prometheus down as best I could. Then I took off. As I drove down the Underworld Highway, I thought about the Titan's boast to bring fire to the guys. The only way he could get it was to steal it from Mount Olympus. My sister Hestia is the Olympian guardian of fire. She tends an everlasting flame at her hearth. Every morning, it's a tradition for all the gods who live on Mount Olympus to bring a torch to Hestia's flame. They hold it to her fire and light it. (Except for Zeus, who always sends his Serving Nymphs to get his fire for him.) Then they take their fire back to their palaces to be used for heating and cooking. The fires die down during the night. So the next morning, everyone comes back to

Hestia for a light. Being goddess of the hearth isn't a huge job. But Hestia takes it very seriously. She watches her flame like a hawk. She'd never give fire to Prometheus. So Part II of his plan would never happen. That was too bad for the guys. But it was good for Prometheus, because it kept him safe from the wrath of Zeus.

Back in the Underworld, things were shaping up. Cerberus was catching on to my "No bark!" command. And I was teaching him to play "Catch the Discus." He was good at it. After all, with three heads, he had triple the chance of catching it. Sometimes, though, two or even three of Cerbie's heads started fighting over the discus. Then there was plenty of snapping, snarling, growling, and barking. Luckily, it didn't happen very often.

One day I clipped my Helmet of Darkness to my belt and walked Cerbie all the way to the Styx. I had Charon ferry Cerbie and me across the river so we could play fetch on the opposite bank for a change. (The old money-grubbing ferryman charged one gold coin for me and triple for the dog!) This riverbank was where I'd first laid eyes on Cerbie. He was a little three-headed pup then. And it was the place where he'd come to me with a note from his mother tied to his collar. The note said that Cerbie wanted to be my dog. So this riverbank was a special place for me and my pooch.

I threw the discus. Cerbie caught it and ran to me. As we played, Hermes's old rattletrap of a bus rounded the last curve of the Underworld Highway and clattered onto the riverbank.

"Cerbie, come!" I called. Hermes is a reckless driver, and I wanted Cerbie out of his way.

The bus screeched to a stop in front of Charon's ferry. The messenger god hopped out of the driver's seat. I expected to see a load of ghosts pile out of the bus after him. But there were none. Hermes flapped the little wings on his helmet and sandals and flitted over to me.

"Greetings, Hades," said Hermes.

"Greetings," I said, staring at the empty bus. "Where did the ghosts go?"

"I didn't bring any," Hermes said. "I'm here strictly in my role as messenger of Zeus."

I groaned. "What now?"

"He wants you up on Mount Olympus," said Hermes. "There's some sort of big emergency. Come on. I'll give you a lift."

I groaned again. Nine days and nights to get up to earth! And nine more to get back. Even for an immortal, it was a nightmare. But what choice did I have? Zeus was a cheat and a total myth-o-maniac. But surely he wouldn't have sent Hermes for me unless it was a real emergency. Maybe at last he realized that he needed the advice of his wise older brother. I picked up the dog and followed Hermes to his old bus.

"Let's go," I told him.

CHAPTER VII
WERE THE GUYS COOKING STEAKS?

"Hades," said Hermes. "You can't bring a dog on my bus."

"I can't leave him on the riverbank," I said. "Don't worry about it. He's very well behaved." I sat down behind the driver's seat and put Cerbie on the seat next to me. "Ready when you are."

Hermes revved his engine, did a U-ie, and began chugging up the Underworld Highway. I tried to get comfortable. But if you've ever spent any time riding a school bus, then you know that's impossible. Cerbie snoozed for a few hours. Then he woke up, full of pep. He started racing up and down the aisle.

"I thought you said he was well behaved," said Hermes, shooing him away.

"Maybe he has to go," I said. "Pull over, Hermes. Let me take him for a little walk."

Hermes stopped the bus. He opened the door. Cerbie leaped out and took off running.

"Hey, Cerbie! Stop!" I cried. "Come! Sit! Stay!"

But Cerbie ran until he was out of sight.

I ran after him, through the woods, calling and whistling. I chased that dog for nearly an hour. I chased him up the mountain that stands between earth and the Underworld. Why wouldn't he stop? Maybe he was a barker. But he'd never run away before. He always stuck to me like glue. What was wrong?

Finally, Cerbie slowed down. Then he flopped to the ground, panting in triplicate.

I was panting myself by then. I managed a "Good boy, boy, boy. Stay! Staaay . . ." But just as I reached for him, he sprang up and raced off.

And I raced after him.

He played this little trick a dozen times.

"Cerbie!" I wailed. "Don't run away from me!"

But he kept going. At last he ran into the mouth of a cave. I followed him.

"Cerbie!" My voice echoed through the cave.

"Rrrrruff!" Cerbie barked.

I couldn't see him. But I could hear him panting. I followed the sound deeper and deeper into the cave. If I ever caught him, I vowed to fence in part of my yard. I'd never take him out with me again. He'd see what happened to dogs who didn't come when they were called.

Then, to my utmost amazement, I followed him out of the dark cave into bright sunlight.

Cerbie sat down in front of me, panting happily.

I looked around. I couldn't believe my eyes.

"Cerbie?" I said. "Did you just show me a secret shortcut from the Underworld to earth?"

"Yup!" Cerbie barked. He looked very pleased with himself.

"Good dog, dog, dog!" I praised him, patting each of his heads. "Cheese Yummies for you tonight. All you can eat!"

Cerbie had changed my life. From that day on, my trips up to earth took a few hours instead of a grueling nine days. What a pooch!

Just then I remembered Hermes. Was he still sitting in his bus, waiting for me to come back with my dog? I thought about going back for him. But Zeus had sent him to get me. He wanted me, on the double, to solve whatever problem he was up against. Zeus needed me. Hermes could wait. I picked up Cerbie and quickly chanted the astro-traveling spell. *ZIP!* I landed just outside Zeus's palace on the top of Mount Olympus.

I put Cerbie down. He spotted Demeter's little dog, Sproutsie, and ran off to play with her. Just as well, I thought. Zeus was probably wouldn't let him into the palace anyway.

I started up the palace steps. But at the door, two big, mean-looking guys with shaved heads blocked my way.

"Name?" said one.

"Hades," I told them.

"Got a picture ID?" asked the other. "An oil painting of yourself is best. But a charcoal sketch will do."

"I'm Zeus's brother. His older, wiser brother. He sent for me," I explained.

The door opened. Zeus stuck his head out. "Hades!" he said. "I didn't expect you so soon." He nodded to one of the bruisers. "Call the others, will you, Force? We can start the meeting now."

Force? What sort of name was *that*? I followed Zeus into the palace. "Who are those two?" I asked.

"My bodyguards," said Zeus. "Force and Violence. Come on, Hades. Time to start the meeting."

"Bodyguards?" I said. "Since when do you need bodyguards?"

"You never know," said Zeus. "The universe can be a dangerous place."

I followed him into his conference room. A gigantic portrait of him hung on a wall. Under it a brass plaque read:

ZEUS, ALL POWERFUL THUNDER GOD, RULER, AND C.E.O. OF THE UNIVERSE.

All the Power Olympians began filing into the conference room. (Except for Hermes, who was probably still somewhere on the Underworld Highway.) Naturally lots of Zeus's kids showed up. Force and Violence closed the big double doors and stood in front of them. Creepy.

We all sat down at the table. Po sat across from me. He gave a nod.

"Let's get started," said Zeus. He didn't seem to notice that Hermes was missing. "Here's the situation. A few nights ago, I was flying over earth in my sky chariot. Earth is dark at night. Except if a volcano is erupting. Or if I hurl one of my mighty T-bolts and light things up. Or if I —"

"Zeus," Hera cut in. "This isn't about you."

"Of course it is," muttered Zeus. "What I'm saying is, the earth, which is part of the universe, which I rule —" he glared at Hera to prove his point — "is pitch-black at night. That's because mortals do not have lanterns or candles or any of those things, because they don't have *fire*. Or didn't," he added darkly, "until now."

Oh, no! had Prometheus somehow carried out Part II of his plan? Had he stolen fire for the guys?

"So I steer my steeds in for a landing," Zeus went on. "And what do I see? I see torches! I see cooking fires! And campfires! And guys sitting around them, toasting *marshmallows*!"

"Were the guys cooking steak?" asked Aphrodite.

"They were grilling 'em!" said Zeus. "Grilling steaks that, by rights, belong to us gods!"

"How did the guys get fire, Dad?" asked Athena.

Zeus turned to Hestia. "Go on, Hestia. Tell what happened."

Hestia rose to her feet, rather reluctantly. "A while back, I was tending my hearth," she began. "And Prometheus stopped by to see me."

"How did a Titan get onto Olympus anyway?" asked Po.

Zeus turned to Athena and raised an eyebrow.

"Okay, I let him in the back way," Athena confessed. "He and the other Titans used to live up here on Mount Olympus. He told me he wanted to look around at his old home. I didn't think there was any harm in it."

Zeus nodded to Hestia to continue.

"Prometheus came by," she said. "He was carrying a big stalk of fennel."

"Fennel," put in Demeter, goddess of agriculture, "for those who don't know, is a licorice-scented vegetable. It has feathery green leaves and a long celery-like stalk, with a big bulb at its base. It is excellent roasted or in soups, salads, and —"

"Demeter!" snapped Zeus. "Enough!" He turned to Hestia. "Go on."

"I should have asked Prometheus why he had the fennel," Hestia admitted. "But at the time, it just didn't seem that strange. Zeus, you always carry a bucket of thunderbolts. Po, you always carry that big three-pronged spear. Demeter, you carry a trowel. So I figured Prometheus carried fennel. How was I supposed to know it wasn't his special thing?"

"The point, Hestia!" shouted Zeus. "Get to it!"

Hestia sniffed. "Prometheus was very friendly. He sat down beside me, asked how I was. No one ever does that. All the rest of you immortals are always sooooo busy. You pass right by me sitting at the hearth. Half the time you don't even say hello. But Prometheus stopped. He sat down. He seemed interested in what I had to say," she added, her voice cracking a bit.

"Tell what happened!" thundered Zeus.

Hestia pushed a strand of hair out of her eyes. "I noticed that Prometheus had set the fennel down very close to the coals. Well, it was *in* the coals, actually. But as I said, I didn't think that much of it. And it smelled good as it smoldered. We talked for a while. Then Prometheus said he had to go. He scooped up the fennel stalk, and off he went."

"I'm still confused," said Hera. "What does this have to do with the mortals getting fire?"

"I guess Prometheus must have hollowed out the fennel bulb before he came to see me," Hestia said. "And when he picked it up from the hearth, he must have scooped up some of my red-hot coals." She sniffed again.

I felt bad for Hestia. She'd let the Titan sweet talk her into neglecting her hearth.

"Now Prometheus has given fire to those stubby mortals he made," Zeus said. "Now they don't have to live in caves to keep warm anymore. Now they're making tools and bowls and beach umbrellas. They're building houses and grocery stores and bowling alleys. Next thing you know, they'll be wanting to buy resort property on Mount Olympus!"

Did I mention that Zeus is also the king of exaggeration? Yet he didn't seem quite as angry about the guys having fire as I thought he'd be.

"Prometheus gave the guys the gift of fire." Zeus smiled maliciously. "Now *I* have a gift for the guys." He turned and nodded to Force and Violence. They swung open the door. "Hephaestus?" called Zeus. "Bring in Pandora!"

CHAPTER VIII

WHAT CAN YOU GIVE PANDORA?

Pandora? What was Zeus talking about?

I watched, fascinated, as Hephaestus limped into the room, pulling a wheeled platform. Whatever was on it was draped with a cloth.

Hephaestus walked slowly, so it took him some time to pull the platform to the center of the room. Hephaestus is the son of Hera and Zeus. As you know, those two are always bickering. Once, when Hephaestus was young, his parents started quarreling. Hephaestus spoke up. He sided with Hera. Big mistake! Zeus got angry. He picked up Hephaestus up and flung him so hard and so high that he sailed off Mount Olympus and fell for a whole day. At last he came down on the island of Lemnos. He landed hard, stubbing the big toe of his left foot, and he's limped ever since.

The sea goddess Thetis found Hephaestus lying on the sand, holding his foot and whimpering. She bandaged his toe, but there was nothing she could do it fix it. Finally, Hephaestus limped home to Olympus. Father and son forgave each other. Zeus even said Hephaestus could marry Aphrodite, the goddess of love and beauty. Aphrodite wasn't all that crazy about the idea. But she agreed because she was crazy about the gold jewelry Hephaestus made at his forge, this great, huge, hot furnace. When Zeus saw how talented Hephaestus was at his forge, he made him the god of fire. Hephaestus made the thrones for all the Olympians. He's an excellent sculptor, too. I wondered what he'd made now.

"All right, Hephaestus." Zeus rubbed his hands together with glee. "Let's see what you've got."

"Heeeeere's . . . Pandora!" Hephaestus yanked off the cloth. On the platform stood a white marble statue of a young goddess. She was smaller than a real goddess. But just as beautiful. She looked a lot like Aphrodite. Hephaestus had made her lips from red rubies. Her eyes were blue sapphires. He'd carved her head so that it looked as if her hair were pulled back into a knot at the nape of her neck.

All at once, Zeus started shouting. "You dunderheaded lout! You muddle-skulled nincompoop!"

"Who, *me*?" said Hephaestus.

"Yes, you!" roared Zeus. "I have a mind to pick you up and hurl you to the ends of the universe!"

"Why?" Hephaestus looked truly puzzled. "You told me to make a statue of a beautiful goddess. Only smaller. And that's what I did!"

I was so confused as Hephaestus. Why was Zeus so angry? And why did he want to give a statue to the guys?

"You were supposed to make it out of the clay from the bank of the River Asopus!" shouted Zeus.

"But marble is better than clay!" said Hephaestus.

"Not the clay I'm talking about," said Zeus.

"That clay has sparks of life in it! It's what Prometheus used to make his mortals. That's how they came to life. You think marble can come to life?"

"Guess not," muttered Hephaestus. "Sorry, Dad."

"You didn't know, honey!" Hera called out to her son. "I'm sure your daddy wasn't clear about what he wanted. His communication skills are terrible."

I was catching on. Zeus had wanted Pandora to come to life. Then he'd send her down to earth. She'd meet the guys. Only one of her among all those guys. The old schemer knew that would cause trouble.

"Take her away!" Zeus was shrieking. " I never want to see that hunk of cold stone again as long as I —" He stopped. A gleam came into his eyes. "Wait. Maybe there's another way. Yes! The winds can breathe life into Pandora." He turned to his bodyguards. "Force! Violence! Get me the winds. All four of them. I mean now!"

The bodyguards hurried from the room. They

hadn't been gone long when the door blew open, and a warm gust of air breezed in.

"It's me, Zephyr," said a breathy voice. "West Wind, at your service."

"Where are the other winds?" shouted Zeus. "Why aren't they here?"

"Don't get your toga in a twist," said Zephyr. "First tell me what you want."

"I want the winds to breathe life into that!" Zeus pointed at Pandora.

I felt Zephyr blowing gently around the statue. "Well, well, who have we here?"

"Pandora!" said Zeus. "Listen, Zipper. Call your brothers. Let's get moving here!"

A breeze rippled through the room. "He doesn't even know my name," said Zephyr. "But he wants me to help him." Suddenly Zeus's hair begin to blow all over the place. It made a mess of his comb-over and revealed his bald spot. It was bigger than I'd remembered.

"Somebody had better remember to drink his daily nectar, or he's going to be as bald as a baby's bottom," said Zephyr, still gusting.

"Hey, cut it out!" Zeus said. He clapped a hand on top of his head and tried to smooth his hair back into place.

"I can take care of this for you solo, Zeus," said Zephyr. "I don't think you want my brothers up here on peaceful Mount Olympus anyway. Boreas, the North Wind, will make you shiver. Notus, the South Wind, will blow through here like a hurricane. Eurus, the East Wind, is a tornado specialist. I'd hate to see your palace after they blew into town."

"All right!" cried Zeus. "Enough talk! If you can do it, get to work!"

All the gods grew quiet, waiting. I thought Zephyr might have to blow up a strong wind to bring a marble statue to life. But she didn't work that way.

Puff!

Pandora blinked her sapphire eyes.

Another *puff!*

She twitched her nose.

And so it went, puff by puff. Color came into Pandora's cheeks. Her robe turned from stone to cloth. And her hair that had been carved from marble turned to shiny black tresses.

Finally: *Puff!*

Pandora's ruby lips curved up in a smile. She turned her head. She seemed to see us. But she had a blank look on her face, as if she weren't quite finished.

"She's alive," said Zephyr. "But empty as a satyr's wine jug. Well, my part's done. Don't bother thanking me, Zeus. I might faint from surprise."

"Just go," said Zeus, shooing her with both hands. "Go, go, go!"

And Zephyr blew away.

"That worked great, Dad," said Hephaestus. "*Now* do you like my statue?"

But the old myth-o-maniac didn't bother to answer. He hurried over to Pandora. "Hello there, sweetheart!" he said.

"Will you look at that," said Hera. "Two minutes ago, she was a hunk of rock. And now he's flirting with her!"

Zeus held out a hand and helped Pandora

step down from the platform. She stood gazing at him with a small, meaningless smile.

Zeus turned to us. "It's up to us Olympians to finish her. The name Pandora means 'everybody gave me a real nice gift.' So give her gifts. You get the idea. Hera, you go first. Start things off. What can you give Pandora?"

CHAPTER IX

DID YOU HEAR THE ONE ABOUT THE CHICKEN?

Hera rose and walked over to Pandora. "As goddess of marriage," she said, "I give you the gift of a very long and very happy marriage." She tapped Pandora on the top of the head.

Smart move, I thought. If Pandora were happily married, she wouldn't be interested in being wooed by Zeus.

"I'd better go next," said Athena, goddess of wisdom. "She needs some brains." She, too, came over to Pandora. "I give you the gift of good judgment," she said, tapping Pandora's head. At that touch, Pandora's eyes lit up. The blank look vanished.

Athena smiled. "I think I'll call you a . . . girl."

"I'll go next," said Apollo. "I want to hear the girl say something." He went up to her. "Pandora, I give you the gift of a lovely voice." He tapped Pandora's head. *Tap!*

"Thank you," said Pandora. Her voice was sweet and musical.

It was thrilling to see Pandora come to life this way. And so far, so good on the gifts. Pandora was getting nicely set up. Good marriage, good judgment, lovely voice. But things went rapidly downhill from there.

Hestia popped up. "Pandora, as goddess of the home, I give you a gift every homemaker needs: the ability to get out any stain!" *Tap!* "Even grape juice!"

"Thank you," said Pandora.

Now it was Po's turn. "I am god of the seas," he said. "Also a major party god. If you ever want to know where the action is, just call —"

"Get to the gift!" bellowed Zeus.

"Okay, okay," said Po. "Pandora, you're a great party giver!" *Tap!* "And, hey! When you have a bash, don't forget to invite ol' Po!"

"You'll be first on my list," said Pandora.

"And," said Po, " I'd also like to give you the gift of looking great in a bikini!"

"One gift!" Hera called out. "You're done, Po."

"Aw, come on!" said Po. "I was just getting started!"

"Demeter!" shouted Zeus. "You're up."

Demeter stood. "Any plant you tend will grow lush and have many blossoms," said the goddess of agriculture. "For I give you the gift of a green thumb." *Tap!*

Instantly, the thumb on Pandora's left hand turned bright green.

Everyone in the room gasped.

Demeter looked horrified. "It's a saying!" she said. "I didn't mean for it to turn green."

"Too bad," said Zeus. "Next!"

But before anyone could speak, there was a knock at the door. Violence peeked through the crack to see who was there. Then he opened the door, and Hermes flew in.

"Thanks for deserting me, Hades," he said as he darted into the conference room.

"How did you get up here so fast?" I asked.

"I followed you," Hermes said. "Think it was easy in a bus? But it was worth it. Because now I know —"

"Shh!" I put my finger to my lips. I didn't want everyone in Olympus knowing there was a shortcut down to the Underworld. Think of the drop-in company! "Let's keep it between us, okay, Hermes?"

"Maybe," said Hermes. "We'll talk. Make a deal." He sat down, and Hera filled him in on what was happening with Pandora.

"I've got a gift for you, Pandora." He jumped up and flew over to her. He reached into the little pouch he always carried and pulled out a pair of sandals. They had tiny silver wings on the heels.

Pandora buckled on the sandals. She seemed pleased.

"The wings don't work," Hermes told us. "They're decorative. I'm thinking of going into the fashion business. What do you think, Dad? Really primo leather goods with my name on them?"

"Fine, fine, whatever," said Zeus. "Aphrodite?"

The goddess of love and beauty sprang from her chair.

"*Cara mia!*" exclaimed Aphrodite, ever eager to sprinkle a bit of Italian into any conversation. "My dear!" She tottered over to Pandora on her high-heeled sandals. She kissed her fingers and blew the kiss. "*Pandorina!* I need not give you the gift of *la belleza* — beauty. That you already have. Perhaps a touch too much," she murmured with a quick glare at Hephaestus. Then she caught herself and smiled. "So I give you all the extras: long nails, perfect skin, and the gift of *capelli interessante*!"

"Hey! No fair!" called Po. "She's giving more than one gift!"

Zeus ignored him.

Pandora's nails grew, and her skin took on a rosy glow. I wasn't sure what *capelli interessante* meant. But it had something to do with hair, for Pandora's hair was undergoing a remarkable change. First the color turned from shiny black to hot pink. Then it burst from the knot at the nape of her neck and began whipping wildly around her head. *Whap! Whap! Whap!* When the last strand whipped into place, Pandora's hair looked like a cross between a wasps' nest and a battle helmet. Two little tendrils popped out on the sides and corkscrewed down over each ear.

"There!" Aphrodite smiled. "Now, *cara mia*, you are finished. *Finita!*"

Poor Pandora. She was finished, all right. Finished for any competition with Aphrodite in the looks department.

"Hey, Dad!" called Thalia, the muse of comedy. "Can I give the girl a gift?"

"No!" Zeus thundered loudly. "You're a lowly muse. Gifts are to be given by gods and goddesses only."

"Lighten up, Dad," said Thalia. "You'll get a kick out of this one."

"Oh, all right," said Zeus. He never could resist his own children. "But be quick about it!"

Thalia approached the former statue. "Here's my gift, Pandora: the ability to tell a great joke!" She touched Pandora's hairdo. *Tap!*

Pandora's eyes lit up. "Say, Thalia, did you hear the one about the chicken?"

"Save the jokes!" snapped Zeus. "Let's finish up here. Anyone else?"

No one else volunteered.

Pandora could only be the sum of her gifts. So that made her a joke-telling party hostess with great skin and nails, sound judgment, a lovely voice, a green thumb, and nice sandals, who could get out any stain and would someday be happily married. Whew! I thought there was a good chance that the girl was going to end up with a bad case of multiple-personality disorder.

"I have a gift for Pandora," I said. I rose and walked over to her. I had something I figured she could use no matter how bad things got. I put my hand on her hot-pink hair.

"As god of the Underworld, I am also god of wealth," I said. "And here's my gift for you, Pandora. You'll always be able to make a good living." *Tap!*

"Thank you," said Pandora.

"My turn!" said Zeus. "I've saved the best

for last." He hurried over to Pandora, smiling as though someone had given him the gift of cunning. "Here's my gift, sweetheart," he said. He put his hand on Pandora's head. "I give you the gift of curiosity. Extreme curiosity!" *Tap!*

"Why Zeus?" said Pandora. "Why? It there a reason you chose that particular gift?"

"You'll see, sweetheart," said Zeus. Now he handed her a box.

"Is this for me?" asked Pandora as she took it.

"No, sweetheart," said Zeus. "I want you to deliver it to someone for me. But whatever you do, don't take the lid off and look inside!" Then Zeus burst out laughing like a maniac.

CHAPTER X

WHAT'S INSIDE THE BOX, ZEUS?

"Hermes!" yelled Zeus. "Take Pandora down to earth to see Epi."

"Aw, Dad! Give me a break!" said Hermes. "I just got here."

"Hermes . . ." said Zeus in a warning tone.

"All right, all right," said Hermes.

"Pandora, when you meet Epi, give him the box," said Zeus. "Say it's a gift from Zeus. But on your way, don't open it. Got that?"

Hermes rose from his chair. He activated his helmet and sandal wings and flapped over to Pandora. "Come on, Pandy," he said. "Let's go find Epi."

"Who is Epi?" said Pandora as Hermes tried to escort her from the conference room. "What makes you think that I would enjoy meeting him?"

"Oh, and sweetheart?" Zeus called loudly after Pandora.

Pandora stopped and turned to face him.

"The box!" Zeus called. "Remember, now — don't open it!"

"Why are you telling me again, Zeus?" asked Pandora.

"Just want to make sure you understand," he said, winking broadly at the rest of us. "Don't even lift the lid a teensy bit and peek at what's inside."

"Why would I do that, Zeus?" she asked. "Did you not just tell me not to?"

"Go," said Zeus, shooing her and Hermes away. "Go, go, go."

Off they went. I supposed they'd ride down to earth in Hermes's rattletrap bus. Not a great way to make an entrance.

When they had gone, Zeus pumped a fist in the air. "Yes!" he shouted. "Pandora won't be able to resist opening that box. And even if she does, Epi will open it. Hee-hee! Then Prometheus and those squatty mortals of his will really be in for it!"

"What's inside the box, Zeus?" said Hera.

Zeus grinned menacingly. "Lots of good stuff."

"Like what, Dad?" asked Athena.

Now everyone had extreme curiosity. Even me.

"You'll see." Zeus was practically glowing with happiness at his latest scheme. He caught my eye and waggled his bushy eyebrows. "Hades? Do you think the curious girl will open the box?"

"You told her not to," I said. "I don't think she'll peek."

"No-o-o-o-o-o-o!" said Zeus. "She'll peek! I'll put money on it!"

I only shrugged.

"You're smart, Athena," said Zeus. "What do you think?"

"I'm wise, Dad," said Athena. "That's even better than smart. And do I think she'll open the box? Probably."

"Yes!" said Zeus. "Everybody else thinks so,

too, right?" He looked around the conference room. "Hestia? Po?"

They nodded.

Now Zeus turned back to me. "It's just you, Hades," he said. "You're the only one who thinks she won't peek. Are you ready to put your money where your mouth is? I'll bet you she will. I'll bet however much you say."

"I don't want to bet, Zeus," I said.

"Come on, Hades," said Zeus. "I'll put ten million dekadollars on it."

A dekadollar is worth ten of your mortal dollars. You do the math. We were talking big bucks here.

Zeus was practically jumping up and down, he was so excited. "Take the bet, Hades," he said. "What are you afraid of? That I'm right? I know I am!"

He kept up his chattering. Finally I held my hand up in surrender.

"Fine, Zeus," I said. "I'll take the bet. Ten million dekadollars says she won't open the box."

"You're all witnesses!" Zeus cried to the other gods. "Hades took the bet." He started laughing again.

My Zeus-tolerance was wearing thin. "If there's nothing else to take care of here," I said, "I'll get back to my kingdom."

"Bye, Hades!" called Po.

"See you, Hades!" called Hera.

All the other gods and goddesses waved.

I left the conference room. Zeus shouted after me, "So long, sucker!"

Once I was outside the palace, I called for Cerbie.

"That's my boy!" I said, when he and Demeter's dog came running. "Tell Sproutsie goodbye." I picked him up. Shortcut or no shortcut, I didn't want to walk back to the Underworld, so I chanted the astro-traveling spell. *ZIP!* I landed at Midas Rent-a-Chariot, not far from the foot of Mount Olympus.

I'd just started off in what passes for a chariot at Midas's, when I heard the squeal of tires. There was Hermes's rattling old bus making the last turn down from Mount Olympus. With a screeching of brakes, the bus pulled over to the side of the road. The door opened, and Pandora practically leapt out. She stood beside the bus, holding her box with one hand and her stomach with the other.

"Why did you not slow down when I asked you to, Hermes?" Pandora looked very queasy. "Why did you have to drive so fast and make me feel so sick?"

"Sorry about that," said Hermes, as he, too, got out of the bus. "Usually, I'm by myself on this road, so I go pretty fast."

"Can we walk the rest of the way to where we are going, Hermes?" asked Pandora.

"It's too far," said Hermes. "Come on, Pandy. Pull yourself together. Get back in the bus so I can take you to Epi's house."

"Hermes?" said Pandora. "Did you hear the one about the chicken?"

Pandora was playing for time. She needed help.

Quickly, I pulled my wreck of a chariot

into the bushes. I unclipped my Helmet of Darkness from my girdle and put it on. *POOF!* I disappeared. I made my invisible way over to Pandora and Hermes, figuring I'd know what to do when the time came.

"Get into the bus, Pandora," Hermes was saying.

"Hermes?" said Pandora. "Do you think Epi has heard the one about the chicken?"

"I wouldn't know," Hermes told her. "Get back on the bus, will you?"

I heard footsteps. I turned and saw a stranger approaching. He wore glasses, which was very unusual for those days. He had a big nose and a ratty-looking mustache. He was bigger than a guy. But he didn't look like a god, either. None of the gods had bad eyesight. None of the gods had big noses or ratty mustaches, either. There was something weird about this stranger. But also something familiar.

The stranger walked up to Pandora. "Hello, there," he said. "Say, that's a fine-looking box you're holding. What's in it?"

Pandora looked at the stranger curiously.

"Are you asking me to open this box?" she said.

"That's right, sweetheart." The stranger's eyes lit up behind his glasses. "Open it."

Sweetheart?

Suddenly it hit me like a ton of phony noses.

The stranger was Zeus!

CHAPTER XI

DO I WIN A PRIZE?

"Why, stranger?" said Pandora. "Why do you want me to open this box?"

"Just do it, sweetheart," Zeus-in-disguise said.

That Zeus would stoop to this to win a bet shouldn't have surprised me. But it did. I shouldered invisibly closer to the big cheater. I gave him a nudge. He lost his balance, and his glasses, nose, and mustache went flying.

"Whoa!" cried Zeus, reaching out and trying to catch them.

Pandora's eyes widened. "Why has part of your face fallen off, stranger?" she asked.

"Dad?" said Hermes. "Is that you?"

The "stranger" quickly scuttled away, trying to keep his face hidden.

Pandora turned to Hermes. "Was this unusual?" she asked.

"You could say that," said Hermes. "Come on, Pandy. Back on the bus."

Pandora winced. "Is there no other way I can travel to meet Epi?"

"Nope," he said. "The bus is the only way."

I made a fast decision. I took off my helmet. *FOOP!* I appeared before them.

Hermes jumped back, startled. "Hades!"

"Where did you come from?" asked Pandora.

"It's the helmet," I told her. I gave a little demonstration. "I put it on, and I disappear." *POOF!* "I take it off, here I am." *FOOP!* "Listen, I have a chariot parked right over there. Would you like me to give you a ride to Epi's house, Pandora?"

Pandora turned to Hermes. "Would you mind terribly?"

"No!" said Hermes quickly. "I mean, whatever you want to do."

She turned back to me. "Can you take me, Hades?"

"Be glad to," I told her. And I walked with her over to the chariot.

"Are you a guard dog?" Pandora asked Cerbie, patting each of his heads in turn. It was evidently the right thing to say. Cerberus triple licked her hand and voluntarily jumped into the backseat.

"Oh, has the dog left a stain on your upholstery?" said Pandora, rubbing a spot on the seat with her bright green thumb. "Do you want to me try to get this out? Do you have any club soda?"

"Don't worry, it's a rental," I said. "Climb in!"

She sat down in the front seat, holding the box on her lap.

"Let's go, steeds," I said. Midas had forgotten to tell me their names.

The steeds started down the hill at a nice clip, not too fast, not too slow.

"What is earth like, Hades?" Pandora asked.

"It's pretty much like this," I said, gesturing toward the countryside.

"Who lives here?" asked Pandora.

"Animals," I told her. "And guys."

"What are guys, Hades?" asked Pandora. "Will I enjoy meeting them?"

"Well, that depends," I answered. "Do you like talking about fast chariots and contact sports?"

"Do I?" Pandora shrugged. "Who knows."

I steered my steeds onto a path that wound through the woods. "Now, let me ask you a question, Pandora. Are you curious about what's inside that box?"

"How could I not be?" Pandora asked.

"Are you tempted to open it and find out?" I asked her.

"Do you think I want to break a fingernail, Hades?" asked Pandora. She waggled her shapely fingertips at me playfully.

I smiled. Athena's gift of good judgment seemed to be overpowering Zeus's gift of curiosity.

"Keep a lid on it, Pandora," I said. "That's my advice. Because whatever Zeus has stuffed into that box is bound to be bad news."

"Do you like the gift Aphrodite gave me, Hades?" she asked.

I glanced at her strange, hot-pink hairdo. "Um, well, it's interesting."

She put a hand up and felt her oddly-styled locks. "Is it a good gift, Hades?" she asked.

I didn't want to lie to her. But I didn't want her to feel bad about her looks, either. So I said, "It is the latest thing in hairstyles, Pandora."

That seemed to satisfy her.

"May I ask you a question, Hades?" said Pandora.

She'd already asked me more than a dozen. Why not one more?

"Sure," I said.

"Do you know where I can buy some lovely stationery?" she asked.

"Stationery?" I said. "I don't think it's been invented yet. Why? What do you need stationery for?"

"Don't you think I should write thank-you notes for all of the nice gifts I have received?" Pandora asked.

"Not necessary," I said. "None of the gods are expecting you to do that."

We came out of the woods. Beside the road was a little stand. A crude, hand-lettered sign over it said:

ZORBA THE GREAT
THE WORLD'S BEST GUESSER!
IF I GUESS RIGHT, YOU WIN A PRIZE!

Zorba stood behind the stand. His shaggy hair hung down, hiding his face entirely.

"What is that, Hades?" said Pandora.

"Beats me," I said, slowing the steeds.

"Can we stop, Hades?" asked Pandora. "Can we meet the world's best guesser?"

"Why not?" I said. I was starting to sound like Pandora.

Pandora got out of the chariot, still holding her box. I hopped out, too. So did Cerbie. He immediately started growling. The closer he got to Zorba, the louder he growled.

"Greetings, travelers!" said Zorba. "Oh, what a cute little doggie."

Cerberus let out a triple snarl.

"Cerbie, hush!" I said.

Over Zorba's stand hung an assortment of garishly colored plush animals, cheesy dolls, and cheap beaded jewelry. Among all the glitz was one gold necklace set with a large green stone. Every precious jewel on earth comes from the caves in my kingdom, so I know a thing or two about gems. This was one fine emerald.

"Why are you here?" Pandora asked Zorba.

"Roadside entertainment!" said Zorba. "What can I guess for you today?"

"Can you guess where we are going?" asked Pandora.

Zorba put a hand to his shaggy forehead. "You are going to meet someone," he said. "Yes! Yes! You are going to Epi's house. Did I guess right?"

Pandora nodded. "Do I win a prize?" she asked.

"You win this," said Zorba, pointing to a plush pig. "Or you can let me guess again and try to win a bigger prize. Do you want to do that?"

Pandora nodded. "Can you guess my name?" she asked.

Once more Zorba put his hand to his head. "It begins with a B . . ." he said. "No, wait. Make that a P. Yes! P for . . . Pandora! Did I guess right?"

Pandora nodded again. "What prize do I win now?"

"You can win this pair of fuzzy dice!" said Zorba. "Or, I can guess once more, and maybe you'll win an even better prize."

Pandora eyed the necklace. Athena's gift of good judgment was evidently telling her that it was the real thing.

"Can I go for the necklace?" she said.

"No problem!" said Zorba.

I had to admit it, he was a very good guesser. Cerbie wasn't impressed, however. He had turned down the volume. But he hadn't entirely stopped growling at Zorba.

"I see you are holding a box," Zorba said to Pandora. "May I guess what's inside?"

"Why not?" said Pandora.

This time Zorba put both hands on his head. He swayed and mumbled, as if thinking very hard. "Aha!" he said at last. "I've got it! There's cake in the box. A delicious lemon cake. Did I guess right?"

"How would I know?" Pandora asked.

"You mean you don't know if there's a cake in there or not?" asked Zorba.

Pandora shook her head. "Do I win that necklace?"

"I think so!" said Zorba. "I always guess right! But open the box a teeny bit, will you? Show me the cake to prove that I'm right."

Pandora looked down at the box. She looked back at the world's best guesser. "Zorba?" she asked. "Have you heard the one about the chicken?"

I must have loosened my grip on Cerbie's collar, for suddenly the dog bounded away from me. He ran at Zorba.

"Aaaaah!" the world's best guesser cried as Cerbie lunged at him, knocking him to the ground.

"Cerbie!" I cried. "Stop! Sit! Stay!"

But the dog ignored me. He grabbed Zorba's hair between one of his sets of teeth and ripped it from his head.

I gasped.

There on the ground sat my cheating little brother, Zeus!

CHAPTER XII
YOU GUY?

Zeus quickly chanted the astro-traveling spell. *ZIP!* He was gone.

Pandora stared at the spot where Zeus had been. Then she turned to me. "Hades?" she said. "Why did Zeus pretend to be the world's best guesser?"

"Your guess is as good as mine," I told her. Zeus-in-disguise was getting to be a regular event.

Cerbie had run off into the woods, carrying Zeus's mop of a wig. Now he trotted back without it. He had mud all over his paws. I figured he'd buried the thing.

"Good dog!" I told one head. "Good dog! Good dog!" I told the other two. First he'd showed me a shortcut from the Underworld to earth. Now he'd exposed Zorba as a great big fake. Cerberus was proving to be one useful pooch.

We all got back into the chariot and started off.

"Did you know that that was Zeus all along, Hades?" asked Pandora as we went.

"Well, uh, what do you think?" I said.

Pandora nodded. "Why does this chief god have such strange behavior, Hades?"

"No one knows," I told her. "He was raised by goats. Fairy goats. Maybe that had something to do with it." I was getting worn out from all of Pandora's questions. So I was happy when we reached the sign that said:

WELCOME TO GUYTOWN!
POP. 10,362

I slowed the steeds as we drove through the streets. Things had changed since the last time I'd been here. Then it was a forest, and the guys lived in caves. But now that the guys had fire, they'd figured out how to make stone-cutting tools and bake clay bricks. So the town was full of houses. And driveways. At the end of each driveway stood a long pole with a basket tied to the top. A few guys were throwing stones into the baskets. It looked as if they'd made up another game.

Some guys still wore bark and leaves. Other wore pelts. Still others had wrapped themselves in cloth. It seemed that before long they'd be wearing robes.

Pandora stared at the guys as we went. For once, she didn't ask any questions. But she didn't look too pleased with what she saw.

The guys stared back at Pandora. Long, slack-jawed stares.

I slowed down as we reached two guys walking along the side of the road. They stared at Pandora, too.

"You guy?" one of the guys asked Pandora.

"Pardon me?" said Pandora.

"No!" the other guy answered for Pandora. "No guy have hair like *that*."

"Can you tell me where I can find Epi?" I asked the guys.

"School," said one guy.

"Ah," I said. "And how do I get to the school?"

"Huh!" said one guy. "Real guys not ask directions."

"I'm not a guy," I said. "I'm a god. Gods ask whatever they want. So tell me."

"Okay," said the guy. "Take next left, go to end road, take right. Go II blocks. You there."

"No, go straight," said the other guy. "End of road, take left. You there."

"My way faster!" shouted the first guy.

"My way shorter!" yelled the second.

"Thanks, guys," I said as I left them to their quarrel. Maybe the guys had fire, but they still had a long way to go.

I glanced over at Pandora. She looked horrified. The guys had not made a good first impression.

After a few wrong turns, I pulled up to a big, two-story brick building. Cut into stone above the entry, letters spelled out: **SCHOOL FOR GUYS.**

"Stay, Cerberus!" I said, and left him to guard the chariot.

Pandora took the box and walked with me into the school. A directory inside told where all the classes took place. We stopped to read it:

WOODWORKING	ROOM I
WAGON MECHANICS	ROOM II
METALWORKING	ROOM III
CAMPING SKILLS	ROOM IV
AVOIDING CHORES	ROOM V
DUCK HUNTING	ROOM VI
TOOLS 101	ROOM VII
SHOOTING DARTS	ROOM VIII
CAVE EXPLORING	ROOM IX
FLY FISHING	ROOM X
WEIGHT LIFTING	ROOM XI
PLAYING POOL FOR PROFIT	ROOM XII
ADVANCED GUYS SEMINAR: "THE COUCH POTATO WAY"	ROOM XIII

"Hades?" called a voice from down the hallway. "Is that you?"

I turned. "Epi! We were looking for you."

"Well, you've found me!" Epi smiled. "And who's *this*?" he asked, gazing at Pandora.

"Let me introduce the world's first girl, Pandora," I said.

"Hello, Pandora," said Epi. "Interesting hair!"

"Do you like it?" asked Pandora.

"On you, very much," said Epi. He could be quite charming.

Pandora smiled. "What do you do here at the school, Epi?"

"I'm a teacher," he said. "My subjects are woodworking, darts, and weight lifting."

"Would you like your gift from Zeus now, Epi?" asked Pandora.

"A gift? For me?" said Epi. "Wow! I love presents!" Epi had forgotten all about his brother's warning. And about his promise never to accept a gift from Zeus.

Uh-oh, I thought. But some godly sixth sense told me not to intervene yet.

Pandora handed Epi the box.

"What could it be?" Epi shook the box. Then he started fiddling with the catch.

Pandora tilted her head, watching him. "Epi, do you think it is wise to open a gift from Zeus?" she asked.

Epi stopped. "Hmmmm. You're right." He tucked the gift under his arm.

"Epi," said Pandora, "have you heard the one about the chicken?"

"No," said Epi. "But tell me later, okay? Because I'd like to give you a tour of the school before my next class."

Epi showed Pandora the wood shop, the wagon-mechanics room, the classrooms for Tools 101 and Cave Exploring, and many other classrooms. I followed along behind.

The guys saw Pandora looking into the classrooms at them. They huddled together, muttering, "Who that?" and "Is guy?" and "Not guy!" They couldn't figure her out.

After we'd seen the school, Epi turned to Pandora. "Why don't I take you down to the cafeteria and get you some java? Then you can tell me the one about the chicken."

"Why don't you?" said Pandora.

I could see that the two of them would have more fun without me. "I'll go talk to Prometheus, Epi," I said. "Where is he?"

"Probably in the art room," said Epi. "Up the stairs, straight down the hall, and to the left."

Epi and Pandora went off to the cafeteria. It took me a while to find it, but at last I stumbled into the art room. There was Prometheus, molding a clay guy. He was so intent on his work that he never even noticed me. I waited until he finished his guy. He put him down and looked at him proudly. Only then did he see me.

"Hades!" he exclaimed. "It's been a long time. How do you like Guytown? Things have improved since your last visit to these parts, right?"

"Remarkably," I told him. "I see you're still making guys."

"Yeah, well, I don't need to tell *you* this Hades, but guys are mortal," Prometheus said. "They don't last forever. I have to deep making more to keep things going." He covered his latest clay guy with a cloth to keep him from drying out. He stood up. "So what are you doing here, Hades?"

"I've brought the new mortal that Hephaestus made." I told Prometheus how all the gods and goddesses had given this mortal gifts. "Her name is Pandora," I added. "Athena says she's a 'girl.' She and Epi just went down to the cafeteria."

Prometheus wiped his big hands on a cloth. "I remember Zeus saying that Hephaestus was working on a new mortal." He frowned. "Zeus doesn't have anything to do with the one you brought, does he, Hades?"

"I'm afraid so," I told him. "Zeus gave the new mortal a box. He told her to deliver it to Epi."

"What?" cried Prometheus. The color drained from his face. "Zeus has sent Epi a gift? Why, this is terrible!"

He took off running toward the cafeteria. "Come on, Hades!" he called over his shoulder. "We have to get to him before it's too late!"

CHAPTER XIII
WHAT'S THE TROUBLE?

As I ran down the hallway after Prometheus, I remembered that Zeus had vowed to punish Prometheus. Did this have something to do with the gift he'd sent to Epi?

With his long stride, Prometheus reached the cafeteria before I did. He ran in and right back out again.

"He's not there!" he cried.

Prometheus took off again. I took off after him. We ran all over the school. But there was no sign of Epi.

"Maybe he went home," said Prometheus. I'd never seen the Titan look so concerned.

"I'm parked out front," I said. "Come on. I'll drive you."

We ran out to the chariot and hopped in. Prometheus sat in the back seat with his feet spilling over into the front seat. Even so, it was a tight squeeze for the Titan. Cerbie sat on my lap. The steeds struggled with the weight, but at last they got going and pulled us to Epi's house. It was a grand house, with a large porch across the front. A porch swing hung from the rafters. Epi and Pandora were sitting in it. He had his arm around Pandora's shoulders. The two of them looked very cozy.

Prometheus jumped out of the chariot before I'd reined in the horses. He sprinted up the walk.

I parked and followed him up to the house.

"Epi!" Prometheus said as he leaped onto the porch. "Where is the gift Zeus sent you?"

Epi held up the box. "Right here."

"Oh, good!" Prometheus put a hand to his chest in relief. "You haven't opened it."

"No," said Epi. "I've had other things to think about. Prometheus, this is Pandora."

"How do you do, Prometheus?" Pandora said in her lovely, musical voice.

"So you're the mortal Hephaestus made," said Prometheus. He nodded thoughtfully. "Very nice."

"Would you like to hear some happy news, Prometheus?" asked Pandora.

Prometheus nodded.

"All right," said Epi. "Pandora and I are getting married!"

"Married?" Prometheus stared at his brother in disbelief. "You met, what, twenty minutes ago? And you've already decided to get married?"

"That's right," said Epi.

"Isn't it wonderful?" said Pandora.

"It could be," said Prometheus. "But, Epi, have you thought ahead? Have you considered how this will change your life?"

"Yes!" said Epi. "For once I did think ahead. I love Pandora. I want to marry her and spend the rest of my life with her."

"Psst, Prometheus," I said, beckoning him aside. "Hera gave Pandora the gift of a long and happy marriage. I think they'll be okay."

"All right," said Prometheus. He turned back

to Epi and Pandora. "Then I'm happy for you both. When's the wedding?"

"As soon as I can round up some guys and build a temple," said Epi. "Nothing fancy. A few pillars draped with garlands ought to do."

"Make it big enough so all the guys can come," said Prometheus.

"Will you come to our wedding, Prometheus?" asked Pandora.

"Of course!" said Prometheus. "Now, Epi, about that box. Promise me you'll keep a lid on it. Lock it up someplace, and never, ever open it."

"I promise," said Epi. "The lid stays on."

"Would you like to hear about our wedding plans?" asked Pandora.

"Sure," said Prometheus. He sat down on a bench opposite the swing. "Tell me."

I didn't seem to be needed here. I'd brought Pandora safely to Epi. I was ready to go home to the Underworld. I said my goodbyes, jumped into my chariot, and took off for the shortcut cave.

As I approached the cave, I caught sight of Zeus.

Cerbie did, too. He started growling.

The Ruler of the Universe sat on a rock not far from the mouth of the cave. He was frowning. His nasty-looking bodyguards were messing with one of the wheels on his chariot. Did they know about the shortcut? I hoped not. And they weren't going to find out by watching me drive into the cave. I figured I'd wait until after they'd left. I gave Cerbie the look, and he stopped growling.

"Zeus!" I said as I pulled the chariot up to him. "What are you doing here?"

"Wobbly wheel," said Zeus. "Force and Violence are fixing it."

"I meant, what are you doing here, on earth?" I asked.

"I've just been to the oracle at Delphi, Hades," said Zeus. He looked worried.

I got out of the chariot and walked over to him. Zeus was an obnoxious loudmouth, a cheat, and a bunk-flinging liar. But he was my little brother. Our mom had once made me swear an unbreakable oath on the waters of the River Styx that I would watch out for all my brothers and sisters. Much as I hated to do it, I sat down next to him.

"What's the trouble?" I asked.

"Sibyl," said Zeus. "She's the trouble. You won't believe what she just told me. That someday I'm going to marry a woman who will bear me a son who will overthrow me!"

"Like we overthrew Dad," I said.

"Don't remind me!" shouted Zeus. "It was one thing when we were the teen gods, taking over from the old coot. But now *I* am the old coot." He scowled. "I mean, I don't want any kid of mine taking over!"

"Did the sibyl say anything else?" I asked.

Zeus nodded. "A certain Titan knows the name of the woman who would bear me such an ungrateful son." A crafty look came into his eyes. "If he tells me the name of this woman, then I'll make sure I never marry her. Then she can never bear me such a son. And I'll rule the universe forever!" He was smiling now.

"Which Titan is it?" I asked, fearing that I already knew the answer to this one.

"Prometheus," said Zeus. "He can see into the future. He knows."

Force and Violence started grunting and snorting. It took me a moment to realize that they were laughing.

"We'll take care of Prometheus," Force muttered.

And Violence added, "No problem."

The thugs walked over to Zeus.

"Your chariot is fixed, sir," said Force.

"No more wobbles," said Violence.

"There'd better not be," said Zeus. He stood up. Without so much as a wave goodbye, he climbed into his chariot, and the three of them drove off.

I watched until they were out of sight. I had a bad feeling about what Zeus and Force and Violence were up to. I longed to be back home in the Underworld. But I couldn't go. Not yet. I turned my rental steeds around and galloped back to Guytown.

I had to warn Prometheus.

CHAPTER XIV
I DO?

I galloped back to Epi's house at full
speed. When I got there, I was relieved to see
Prometheus still sitting on the porch, talking to
the happy couple.

"Prometheus!" I called. "I need a word with
you!"

He got up and jogged over to me. "What's
going on?"

"It's Zeus," I said, and I told the Titan about
the sibyl's prediction. "Be on the lookout for
Force and Violence," I warned him. "They're
dangerous."

"Thanks for the warning, Hades," Prometheus
said. "But I can take care of myself." He turned
to go and then turned back. "Oh, by the way,

Hades, Epi and Pandora have set a date for their wedding. Three weeks from today. It'll be here, in Guytown."

"I'll be there," I said. Then I galloped for the shortcut cave. In under four hours, thanks to my pooch, I was back in the Underworld.

That night, I put extra helpings of Underdog Chow in all three of Cerbie's bowls. What a good dog! Without him, I'd still have been on the road.

Three weeks went by in a blur of activity. When the big day arrived, I put on my best robe. I stood in front of my mirror. "An Ambro Bar a day keeps the bald spot away!" I chanted as I combed my thick black hair. Unlike my balding brother, I make sure I get my daily serving of nectar and ambrosia.

When I was looking my best, I turned to my dog. "You stay here and guard my kingdom, Cerbie," I said.

The dog flopped down. He stacked up his heads on his paws, looking lonesome already.

"Don't worry, boy, boy, boy," I said, patting each head. "Thanks to you, I'll be back tonight."

He gave me one little tail wag. But that was all the goodbye I got.

I drove one of my own chariots up to earth, pulling the Midas rental chariot and steeds behind. I returned them and headed for Guytown. After my last experience, I dreaded having to ask directions to the wedding chapel. But luckily, every guy in town was headed in the same direction, so I just followed along. They all streamed into a large white building. Gods were going in, too. And Titans. This was a big, high-powered wedding! I parked and went in with the others.

The Titans were being seated on large benches at the back of the room. I didn't see Mom. That was odd. She loved weddings. I walked down the aisle to the smaller god-sized benches. As for the guys? There were no guy-sized benches. They had to stand in the back. Since the Titans and gods were so much bigger than they were, they wouldn't be able to see a thing. But the guys seemed happy just to have been invited to the wedding.

I sat down on a bench next to my sister Hestia.

"This is so moving," she said, dabbing at an eye with her hanky.

"They haven't even started yet, *cara mia*," said Aphrodite, who sat on her other side. The goddess of L&B looked out of sorts. Had she been hoping that Pandora would ask her to be in the wedding? After her gift of hot-pink hair, that wasn't going to happen.

An organ started to play, and Athena began walking down the aisle. She was followed by Hera, the matron of honor. The music changed to the wedding march. Now Pandora came down the aisle holding Hephaestus's arm. Since he'd created her, it was only right that he should be the one to give her in marriage. Epi and his best Titan, Prometheus, were waiting up by the altar.

Now I caught sight of Rhea. She was in her judge's robe, performing the ceremony! Good old Mom. She made it short and sweet. In no time at all, Epi said, "I do!" Pandora said, "Don't you know I do?" And Mom pronounced them husband and wife. Then everyone went happily into the adjoining banquet hall for the reception.

The first thing I saw in the reception hall was a rickety little card table. On it sat a lone bowl of peanuts in shells. A keg stood beside the card table. All the guys were gathered around it.

Across the room was a long table covered with an elegant white cloth. It was piled high with delicious looking eats. I made my over to it. A sign on the long table said:

FOR IMMORTALS ONLY!

Poor guys, I thought as I helped myself to some nectar punch and giant olive wrapped in smoky ambrosia ham. Sometimes it really pays to be a god. Almost always, actually. I bit into the olive. YUM! I took another. I'm not the world's most sociable god, but I was starting to enjoy myself. So it was a nasty jolt to see Force and Violence hovering nearby. Were they there to keep the guys away from the ambrosia-laced food and the nectar punch? Probably. If mortals consumed any, they'd become immortal.

When I'd eaten possibly more than my share from the wedding buffet, I went to search for Prometheus.

"Excellent wedding," I said when I found him in the crowded room.

"Wasn't it?" said Prometheus. He took a sip of his punch. "I foresee that Epi and Pandora will have many, many children. All girls."

"That ought to make the guys happy," I said.

Prometheus grinned. "I have high hopes that the guys and girls will get along well together," he said.

"Attention! Attention!" called Hera. "The bride will now throw her bouquet!"

Pandora walked halfway up a staircase, holding her flowers. All the single Titanesses, goddesses, muses, graces, and so on gathered at the bottom of the stairs. Everyone else stood back to watch. At the edge of the crowd, I caught sight of Force and Violence.

"Prometheus," I whispered, "watch those two. I have a bad feeling about them."

Prometheus only smiled. "So now you can see into the future, too?"

"I wish," I told him. "Just be careful, will you?"

Prometheus rolled his eyes.

"Is everybody ready?" asked Pandora. And she tossed her bouquet.

Pandora had quite a throwing arm. The flowers arced up into the air. They started coming down right in front of Artemis, the goddess of the hunt.

"It's yours, Artemis!" called Hera. "Catch it!"

"No way!" Artemis jumped away as if the flowers were red-hot coals. "I'm happy being single, thank you very much."

At the last second, Hestia lunged in front of Artemis and caught the bouquet. Everyone clapped, and she burst into happy tears. Then she began to look eagerly around the room.

Still holding the bouquet, she came up to me. "Hades, have you seen Prometheus?"

"I was just talking to him," I said.

"Where is he now?" She stood on tiptoe, looking all around the room.

I looked, too, but I didn't see him. I had a feeling the Titan might have ducked out of the room when he saw who'd caught the bouquet.

"So have you forgiven Prometheus for stealing your fire?" I asked.

Hestia nodded. "It's turned out all right," she said. "And you know, I think he did come up to Olympus at least partly to see me. Well, excuse me for running off, Hades, but I'd really like to find him."

"Go on," I told her.

I caught sight of Mom waving at me from across the room. "Hades!" she called, hurrying over to me. As always, she was carrying two bulging shopping bags. "My firstborn!" she said. "I want to talk to you."

"What about?" I asked. I hoped that it wasn't anything to do with looking after Zeus!

"Weddings, Hades," said Mom. "Don't you think it's time you got married and started giving me some grandchildren?"

I rolled my eyes. (This was long before I met Persephone, my future bride.)

"Aw, Mom," I said. "I'm not the marrying type. Besides, what goddess would want to live down in the Underworld?"

"Don't sell yourself short, Hades," said Mom. "Lots of goddesses would love to be married to a big-time king like you. And don't rule out the muses. Sure, they're minor, as goddesses go. But they are a very talented bunch. They might inspire you!"

"Po isn't married either," I said.

"At least he's dating, Hades," Mom said. "But I want to talk to him, too. Have you seen him?" She surveyed the room.

"There he is. Over by the punch bowl." I felt a bit guilty, giving Po up to Mom like that. But he could handle her.

Mom stared at Po. "Why do you think he streaks his hair blue like that, Hades?"

"Beats me," I said.

"It makes him look so immature." Mom shook her head. "Excuse me, will you?" And she dashed over to the punch bowl.

I watched Mom approach Po. As Po poured

her a cup of punch, I realized that Force and
Violence weren't hovering around the immortals'
table anymore. I did a fast search of the room.
Where were they? And where was Prometheus?
I didn't see him either. I started to get a bad
feeling in my godly gut. A very bad feeling.

I quickly circled the room, looking for
Prometheus. He was the tallest Titan. He'd be
easy to spot. But he wasn't there.

I began looking for Zeus. There he was. He
had cornered a couple of the graces and was
yakking away at them.

I ran over to him. "Zeus," I said, giving him
the nod that I wanted to speak to him.

"Later, Hades," Zeus growled. "Can't you see
we're busy here?"

"Where are those bodyguards of yours?" I
asked him.

Zeus smirked. "I sent them on a mission."

"Does the mission have anything to do with
Prometheus?" I asked him.

"Good guess, Hades!" said Zeus. "You win the
prize!"

CHAPTER XV

HOW COULD I FORGET?

I wasted no time. Right there in the reception hall, I chanted the astro-traveling spell. *ZIP!* I landed on Mount Parnassus, at the entrance to the oracle of Delphi.

Back then, the sibyl was an immortal being. And only immortals consulted her. Since just about all the immortals were at Epi and Pandora's wedding, there was no line, so I walked right into the oracle's cave. I stumbled through the thick yellow smoke, taking care not to step too close to the deep chasm inside the cave. At last I made out the sibyl. She sat perched on a tall three-legged stool balanced at the edge of the chasm. Her eyes were closed.

"Hello?" I whispered, not wanting to startle her. "Sibyl?"

She opened her eyes. They were light blue. She stared at me without any expression on her face. "Speak, pilgrim!" she said in a raspy voice. "What is your question for the oracle?"

"I'm looking for a friend of mine," I told her.

The sibyl closed her eyes again. "Go on," she said.

"Prometheus," I said. "He's a Titan. A big fellow."

"I am aware of the size of Titans," she said.

Oh, great. I'd insulted the sibyl's intelligence. I hoped she wouldn't refuse to give me a prophecy.

"I believe Force and Violence have carried him off," I told the sibyl. "If that's true, then he is in terrible danger. Can you tell me how I can find him? I want to help him."

"You want to find him," said the sibyl.

Now the chasm below the sibyl's stool belched up a huge cloud of yellow smoke. It was so thick, I lost sight of the sibyl. I couldn't see my hand in front of my face. Even breathing was a challenge.

Just when I thought I might pass out for lack of air, the smoke began to clear.

"Pilgrim!" the sibyl cried through the smoke. "The oracle has spoken to me. Hear what it has to say: 'To sail over the turquoise sea, a ship needs what you must seek.'"

"Uh-huh," I said. "Go on."

"I have spoken, pilgrim," said the sibyl. "Be gone!"

I hurried through the smoke out of the cave. I took great big gulps of fresh air. Ahhh! When my head cleared, I sat down on a rock and tried to puzzle out they sibyl's meaning. Was I to get in a ship and sail off to find Prometheus? I said the words over to myself. I asked myself, what does a ship need to sail over a turquoise sea? At once the meaning became clear as . . . the wind.

I chanted the astro-traveling spell again. *ZIP!* This time I landed on the top of Mount Olympus. I figured a high spot must be a good place to call the wind.

"Zephyr!" I called. "I need the help of the wind! Come to me, please!"

I kept calling, and before too long I felt a puff of warm air hit my face.

"Well, well, well," said Zephyr. "A god calls on me for help. What else is new? But at least this one knows the magic word. You think Zeus ever says 'please'? Not in his vocabulary."

"Zephyr," I said. "Thanks for coming."

"Ooooo! Says 'thank you' too! Charming!" Zephyr blew circles around me. "Now what can I do for you, King of the Underworld?"

"It's Prometheus, the Titan," I said. "He's missing."

"Awfully big to go missing," Zephyr said. "But then the world's a big place. I ought to know. I blow around most of it."

"Could you search for Prometheus, Zephyr?" I asked. "As you blow around the world, could you be on the lookout for him? Zeus vowed to punish Prometheus for stealing fire from the gods. I think Zeus's henchmen, Force and Violence, may have kidnapped him."

"Those big bald bruisers?" said Zephyr. "No wonder you're worried. They are bad actors,

those two. If I had an eye, I'd keep it open for
Prometheus. But we winds have other ways. I'll
tell my brothers to search for him, too. If we find
him, I'll bring you word."

"I'll be in the Underworld," I told the West
Wind. "Can you blow down there to find me?"

"Can a duck quack?" she said. "Can a lobster
pinch? Of course I can. I'll find you, Hades,
wherever you are."

"Thank you, Zephyr," I said.

"Don't thank me," said Zephyr, as she blew
away. "I might get used to it."

I didn't know what else I could do to find
Prometheus, so it was *ZIP!* back to my chariot in
the Guytown parking lot. The reception hall was
dark now, the wedding long over. I drove back
to the Underworld. Charon ferried me across the
River Styx. Cerbie was waiting on the far bank to
greet me. He hopped into my chariot, and off we
galloped for Villa Pluto. It was good to be home.

For a time after that, I had no pressing reason
to travel, so I stayed home. Hermes brought the
ghosts of dead mortals down to me in his rickety

old bus. Every week or so, I met him when he arrived, and he told me the news from earth and Olympus. I always asked if anyone had heard from Prometheus. And he always shook his head. It seemed as if the Titan had vanished from the face of the earth.

One day Hermes brought me wonderful news. Pandora had given birth to triplets! Three baby girls. I asked my Cyclopes uncles to make each baby a silver rattle set with little rubies from my kingdom's gem caves. I asked Hermes to take them to the little girls.

Time passed. Hermes brought me the news that Pandora and Epi now had a new set of triplets.

"Girls?" I said.

"Girls," said Hermes.

I sent them silver rattles set with little emeralds.

As the years went by, Pandora and Epi had many sets of triplets. I kept the Cyclopes busy making rattles set with diamonds, sapphires, and every precious stone you can think of. After a while, I lost count of how many girls Epi and Pandora had.

I was happy for them, very happy. But I was still worried about Prometheus. He'd been missing all these years. I'd had no word from Zephyr. What could have become of him?

Often I tossed and turned at night with strange, anxious dreams about the Titan. One morning, after a particularly restless night, I decided to go up to earth and look for him myself.

I threw my Helmet of Darkness into the chariot and hitched up Harley and Davidson. I let Cerbie ride with me as far as the bank of the Styx. Then he jumped out and took his place guarding the gates to my kingdom.

I hadn't been to Guytown in years. I thought it would have changed dramatically. So I was surprised to see that it hadn't changed at all. In fact, fewer guys were on the streets now than before. And lots of them were old guys. Then it hit me. Prometheus wasn't around to make any new guys.

As I drove through town to Epi's house, I saw that the School for Guys was still going. It looked better than the last time I'd seen it. There were curtains in the windows. And the grass and bushes around it were neat and trimmed. The sign above its entry had been changed. Now it read:

SCHOOL FOR GUYS AND GIRLS

I drove until I came to Epi and Pandora's house. Flowers bloomed everywhere, attesting to Pandora's green thumb. There were girls playing in the yard — dozens of them. They were digging in the dirt and hanging by their knees from tree branches. Older girls stood at the edge of the yard, talking to guys. Girls were everywhere! As I walked up to the front door, I saw that two big wings had been added onto the house to accommodate all those girls. I knocked at the front door.

Pandora opened it. She held a baby in her arms. When she saw me, her face lit up. "Hades, is it really you?"

Pandora's hair was still hot pink and wrapped

oddly around her head. She looked a bit older now. And she'd put on weight. Either that or she was expecting more triplets. She looked very beautiful. And very happy.

"Epi?" called Pandora. "Can you come see who's here?"

Epi came in from the rear of the house. He held a baby in each arm. "Hades!" he said. "How great to see you! Come in! Come in!" He led me into their large kitchen. It was clearly the center of their home.

One side of the room had a worn, comfortable looking couch and easy chairs. Several baby girls were crawling around on the floor. And several teenaged girls were looking after them. A clay jar crashed to the floor and broke. When one of the older girls opened a closet to get a broom to sweep it up, a box on a high shelf caught my eye.

"Pandora, is that the box Zeus gave you?" I asked, pointing.

Pandora looked up and seemed half surprised to see it there. "Is it?" she said.

"Yep, that's the box from Zeus," said Epi. "We keep meaning to tie a stone to it and sink it in the sea. But we never seem to get around to it." He shrugged. "When we were first married, Zeus used to show up all the time, trying to coax Pandora to open the box. Do you remember, Pandy?"

"How could I forget?" said Pandora.

"He wore all these crazy disguises," Epi went on. "Once he said he was a chimney sweep. Another time, a window washer."

"Didn't he once pretend to be an exterminator?" asked Pandora.

"Right," said Epi. He shook his head. "He still comes by sometimes. Last time he was dressed as a plumber. Said he'd come to fix the leak. He was messing around in the kitchen for around an hour before we realized that we didn't have a leak, and no one had called a plumber."

"Why does he want me to open the box so much, Hades?" asked Pandora.

"I know one reason," I said. "He made a bet with me. A big bet. If you open the box, Zeus will win the bet, and I'll have to pay. As you can see, he'll do anything to win."

"What do you think is inside the box, Hades?" asked Pandora.

I shrugged. "It's nothing good, that's for sure. Keep a lid on it, Pandora. Don't open it."

A group of girls ran by, yelling loudly. One touched another girl on the head and cried, "You're it!" Then they began running the other way.

"Why don't we sit out on the porch?" said Pandora.

We went back outside. Epi and Pandy sat on the porch swing with their three newest babies. I sat across from them. I could see they were very happy together.

"Did you bring us any news of Prometheus?" asked Pandora.

"No, I was hoping you'd heard something." I shook my head. "I'm going to try to find him, Epi. That's why I've come up to earth."

Two of the older girls brought us lemonade and cookies. Then the babies fell asleep, and the three of us talked about old times. And about all the things that had happened since we'd last seen each other.

"Do you know that I am a teacher now, Hades?" said Pandora.

"I didn't know," I said. "At the School for Guys and Girls?"

Pandora nodded.

"Pandy wasn't all that thrilled when our older girls started hanging out with the guys," Epi told me. "And someday our girls will marry guys. So Pandora took action. She opened the school to girls. And she's added classes for both guys and girls. Classes like 'Expressing Your Feelings' and 'If You Don't Know Where You're Going, It's Okay to Ask for Directions'."

"Don't you think the classes will help make the guys better husbands for our girls?" asked Pandora.

And I told her, "Absolutely."

I felt a gentle breeze blow by. It grew stronger, and stronger and turned into a wind.

"Hades!" said a raspy voice. "I blew all the

way down to the Underworld, looking for you. And here you are, on earth."

"Zephyr!" I exclaimed, jumping up. "Have you found Prometheus?"

"Does a chicken cluck?" said the West Wind. "Does a frog croak? Of course I found him!"

CHAPTER XVI

WHO IS IT?

"Finding Prometheus wasn't easy," Zephyr told us. "It took time. But I'm a patient wind. And persistent, not that anyone appreciates those qualities in me. No, Zeus never mentions how I do nearly impossible tasks for him. Takes it all as his due."

"Zephyr?" said Pandora gently. "Where is Prometheus?"

"He is deep in the rocky Caucasus Mountains," said Zephyr. "He is a prisoner. He cannot escape."

"Oh, my poor dear brother!" wailed Epi.

"Good work, Zephyr," I told her. "No one else could have done what you did."

"Stop!" said Zephyr. "You'll make me blush. Bye, Hades!" And she whooshed away.

"Can you take care of my steeds?" I asked Epi and Pandora.

"The older girls will do it," said Epi.

"Then I will go to the Caucasus Mountains," I told them. "I'll try to free Prometheus. As soon as I can, I'll be in touch with you."

"Good luck, Hades!" Epi called after me as I ran toward my chariot.

"Will you give Prometheus our love?" called Pandora.

"Of course!" I called back as I grabbed my helmet out of the backseat. I put it on. *POOF!* I vanished. I chanted. *ZIP!* Then, *thump!* I landed on a ledge of a Caucasus Mountain peak. Before me stood a huge craggy rock. And bound to the rock with great iron chains was Prometheus. The Titan hadn't heard me land. I walked invisibly around him. Thick iron cuffs bound his wrists and ankles. Heavy chains attached to the cuffs were wrapped around and around the rock. The poor Titan! There was no way he could escape. He could hardly move! Oh, I wanted to shake some sense into my little brother. How could he have done this?

"Prometheus?" I said softly.

The Titan turned his head. "Who calls my name?"

I took off my helmet. *FOOP!*

The Titan saw me and smiled a weary smile. "Hades!" he said. "How good to see a friendly face."

"Force and Violence brought you here, didn't they?" I asked him.

Prometheus nodded. "But please don't say you told me so!"

"I'd never do that," I said.

"Well, you were right," Prometheus said. "I ducked out of the wedding reception. I wanted to practice saying the toast I had planned to give at the dinner."

So he hadn't been avoiding Hestia and her bouquet after all.

"Force and Violence snuck up on me," the Titan went on. "I never heard a thing. They grabbed me and slapped these irons and chains on me. They dragged me out to the parking lot where a pair of huge birds with mortals' faces were waiting. The birds picked me up with their great hooked claws and flew me here to this desolate spot."

"The Harpies?" I asked. "They flew you here?"

"I don't know what those birds are called," said Prometheus. "But they were nasty creatures. And what a foul odor."

"It was the Harpies, all right," I told him. "They're famous for their stench. Some call them the Hounds of Zeus." I looked up at the Titan, chained to the rock. "Do you regret stealing fire for the guys, Prometheus?"

"No!" said Prometheus boldly. "I would do it again if I had the chance. The earth needed guys to live on it. And the guys needed fire to stay warm and to cook and for a hundred other reasons. I'm not sorry I brought them fire. Not at all."

"Brave words," I told him. "But I believe you. Tell me, who brings you food?"

"Force and Violence take turns," Prometheus said. "They unchain one of my hands so I can eat."

"Are they due here soon?" I asked him, looking around.

Prometheus laughed. "You think they come every day? I'm lucky if they come every week. But I get along. My son Deucalion comes when he can. He brings me food and drink. But he has a family. He can't stay with me for long."

"Let me see if I can find a weak link in these chains," I told Prometheus. "I'll try to set you free."

"Don't waste your time, Hades," said Prometheus. "You know I can't often see my own future. But this much came to me in a dream: one day, these chains will be broken. By a mortal, Hades. By a guy! But I must wait for years, for his time has not yet come!"

I whistled. "He'll have to be some big, strong guy, Prometheus," I said. "Whoever Force and Violence got to make these chains didn't mess around."

Prometheus and I talked for a while. I told him about his brother and Pandora and their many, many girls. And about the school. When he heard about the classes Pandora added, he smiled. I could see he was happy that she was taking the guys in hand.

"I guess I can't free you, Prometheus," I said at last. "But can I get you anything? Water maybe?"

"I'd like that, Hades," said Prometheus. "My cup is on the ground, near my feet. There's a stream at the bottom of the mountain."

"I'll be back in a flash." I tucked my helmet under my arm, picked up the cup and astro-traveled to the stream. I filled the cup and was about to return when I heard wings flapping. I hoped with all my godly heart that it was not Harpies' wings. Those birds smelled so bad I didn't see how they could stand to be around themselves. I listened. It wasn't the flapping of big wings. No, it was small wings. But to be on the safe side, I put on my helmet. *POOF!*

I astro-traveled invisibly back to Prometheus. When I saw who'd flown to see him, I gasped. Hermes! What was he doing here?

"Come on, Prometheus," Hermes was saying

to the Titan. "Don't be so stubborn. Just tell me. Who is it?"

"Fly away, Hermes," said Prometheus. "You know I won't tell you her name. Be gone!"

I whipped off my helmet. "Hermes!" I shouted. "You little liar."

"Hades!" Hermes's eyes grew wide when he saw me. "How did you figure out where Prometheus was?"

"I'll ask the questions," I told him. "You've known all along that Prometheus was here, chained to this rock. Didn't you?"

"Maybe," muttered Hermes.

"Every week I met your old bus and asked you for news of Prometheus," I said. "And you always said, 'No news. No one's heard from him. No one knows where he is.'"

"Give me a break, Hades. Dad said I couldn't tell anyone," said Hermes. "I had to keep my mouth shut."

"You lied to me, Hermes," I said. "You're a myth-o-maniac just like Zeus!"

Hermes rolled his eyes. He looked up at the

Titan. "Come on, Prometheus. Spill the beans about who will bear Zeus the son who will overthrow him."

"I'm not talking, Hermes," said Prometheus. "As Zeus would say, end of discussion."

"Please!" Hermes begged. "You've got to tell! If you don't, it'll be . . . awful!"

"What are you saying, Hermes?" I asked. "What will be awful?"

"Zeus really, *really* wants to know who not to marry," Hermes said. He looked away from the Titan. "And he said that if you didn't talk today, he's sending in the eagle."

"The eagle?" said Prometheus.

Hermes nodded. His eyes darted around. I could tell he wasn't enjoying his job as Zeus's messenger. "Um, the one who loves to eat liver," he muttered.

"What do you mean, Hermes?" I asked. I didn't like the sound of this.

Hermes didn't seem to either. He looked sick to his stomach. He had to take several breaths before he finally blurted out, "Tomorrow morning the eagle will come and eat your liver, Prometheus!"

Prometheus only shrugged. "Let him come."

Hermes looked sicker than ever. "Wait," he said. "You haven't heard the worst yet. The night after the eagle eats your liver, it will grow back. But only so, only so —" Hermes clapped a hand over his mouth. He struggled not to be sick, and at last he managed to say, "Only so the eagle can come again the next night and eat it again!"

Hermes ran to the far side of the rock and lost his lunch. I didn't blame him. This was the sickest, most disgusting thing I'd ever heard!

I looked up at Prometheus. I thought he might have passed out from hearing Hermes's words. But the Titan looked stronger and more sure of himself than ever.

When Hermes dragged himself back from the far side of the rock, Prometheus shouted, "Go, messenger of doom! Tell Zeus that even his eagle will never make me talk. I can stand anything he sends me. Neither eagle nor thunderbolt nor

Harpy can drag the name from me! My body may be chained, but my spirit is free!"

Hermes groaned. "Thanks a lot, Prometheus," he said. "When I tell Dad what you said, he's going to be so mad he'll probably hurl a T-bolt at *me*!"

CHAPTER XVII
WHAT'S THIS?

Hermes chanted the astro-traveling spell. *ZIP!*
He was gone. Back to Mount Olympus, no doubt.
I half hoped that Zeus *would* give him a good
scare with one of his T-bolts, the little liar.

An idea came to me then. "I'll be back,
Prometheus," I told the Titan as I held the
cup of water to his lips. "I have to take care of
something right away."

I chanted the astro-traveling spell, too. *ZIP!* I
landed with a thud in my chariot, startling three
of Pandora and Epi's girls who were looking after
Harley and Davidson.

"Hitch up my horses, please!" I told them.
"Quick! And tell your mom and dad I'll be in
touch when I can." The girls expertly hooked

Harley and Davidson to my chariot. I grabbed the reins. "To the Underworld, steeds!" I cried. "And step on it!"

Those horses left a trail of smoke as they sped down to my kingdom. They galloped along the bank of the Styx until they came to an ancient tree. "Whoa, Harley! Whoa, Davidson!" I called, pulling on the reins. They dug in their hooves and skidded to a stop. "Nice going, steeds!" I jumped out of my chariot and gave them quick pats on the neck.

I ran over to the tree. Its branches held an enormous eagle's nest. That nest was the birthplace of every eagle in the universe.

"Ironwings! Brazen!" I shouted up at the nest. "Come down! I need to talk to you!"

A feathered head peered out of the nest. A minute later, a mighty bird flew down and perched on a low branch.

I switched my brain into a godly mode called CCC — which is short for Creature Communication Channel. It's a way we gods have of communicating with any sort of

animal, from flea to whale. I *could* use it to scold Cerbie about his barking. Or to tell Harley and Davidson which way to go. But with my dog and my steeds, I try to keep it simple. A command of "Sit!" A clear "Giddyup!" It's better that way.

But to the eagle, I thought these words: *Greetings, Brazen.*

I greet you, Lord Hades, thought Brazen. *Ironwings is out picking up our dinner. Anything I can help you with?*

I hope so, Brazen, I thought back. And I quickly told her about Prometheus and his endangered liver.

Brazen opened her great hooked beak and stuck out her tongue. *Blech!* she thought. *Who could come up with such a horrible idea?*

Gotta be Zeus, I thought back. *But it's a new low, even for him. Do you have any idea which eagle might be involved in such a nasty plot?*

Zeus keeps several of our offspring up on Mount Olympus, mused Brazen thoughtfully. *But there is only one who might have agreed to this scheme. That would be Clawd.* Brazen shook her feathered head.

He was a bad egg, right from the start. Even as a chick, he was sneaky. Always pecking his nest-mates' feathers and trying to blame one of the others.

What does Clawd like to eat? I thought to her. *Does he have any favorite foods?*

Hot peppers, thought Brazen.

The superhot ones that grow down here in Tartarus? I thought.

Brazen nodded. *Clawd loves them. Even as a chick he liked the spicy bits we regurgitated for him.* She cocked her head to one side. *Shall I have a talk with Clawd, Hades? Let him know his father and I won't put up with him going after anyone's liver?*

That would be excellent, Brazen, I thought. *But he must fly to Prometheus each day. Just as Zeus commanded. We don't want to make Zeus suspicious. Instead of liver for dinner, I'll make sure that he has fresh red-hot peppers from Tartarus. All he can eat.*

Ironwings and I will wing up to Mount Olympus right after dinner, Lord Hades, thought Brazen. *You won't have to worry about Clawd.*

I'm grateful, Brazen, I thought to the eagle. *Very grateful.*

It was a brand-new day in the Underworld by the time I got back to my palace. I ran into the Furies in the kitchen. They'd just gotten home from a night of avenging.

"Winged warriors!" I greeted them. "How did it go up on earth tonight?"

"Good, Hades," said Tisi. "Only one mortal needed our services." The dozens of snakes that sprouted from her head looked wide awake and eager, as if they'd had a good night, too.

It's the Furies' job to hear mortals' complaints about injustice. And to punish any wrongdoer.

"It was a guy," said Meg.

"He was *sassy!*" said Alec. "To his teacher."

"To Pandora?" I asked.

"Yes," said Tisi. "He told her she asked too many questions."

"She *does* ask a lot of questions," admitted Meg. "But only because Zeus gave her the gift of extreme curiosity."

"It's not *her* fault!" said Alec.

"So we punished him," said Tisi.

"He has to write sentences," said Meg.

"'In the future, I shall show respect for my teacher'," said Alec. "Two hundred times!"

"Good punishment, Furies," I said. "Listen, ladies, do you ever fly as far as the Caucasus Mountains?"

"At least twice a week," said Tisi.

"Sometimes more," said Meg.

"*Why?*" said Alec.

So I filled them in on Prometheus. And I told them about Clawd.

"If I got a peck of hot peppers from Tartarus each week, would you be willing to fly it to Prometheus's rock on the sly?" I asked.

"Happy to, Hades," said Tisi.

"Delighted," said Meg.

"*No problem!*" said Alec.

That night I slept soundly for the first time in months. Maybe Prometheus was chained to a rock. Maybe I couldn't save him. But at least I'd saved his liver.

I had a few projects I'd been meaning to do in the Underworld. Now I decided to start. The first thing I did was to put in a pool. When it was finished, I called it the Pool of Forgetfulness. I invited some ghosts to go swimming. I thought it might help them forget their ghostly sorrows. But the water made them forget everything — even how to swim. It was a disaster.

So I built a second pool. This one I called the Pool of Memory, and it worked out much better than the first. I swam in that one from time to time myself.

Up on Mount Olympus, all the gods were getting TVs. So I had the Underworld wired, too. And I got myself a TV for the den. In those early days, there wasn't much on. A talk show or two. Some cartoons. Mostly quiz shows. I became a fan of *Godlywood Squares*. Po was often the center square. What a joker! It was a hoot watching gods making terrible fools of themselves. I found watching TV relaxing after a hard day with the ghosts.

One night I was flipping around the dial. I came across a talk show hosted by a mortal who looked a lot like Pandora. She had the same hairstyle. But she was older. Much older. She could have been Pandora's mother. But of course Pandora didn't have a mother. I didn't want to miss *Godlywood Squares*, so I flipped to it. By the time I flipped back to the talk show, the Pandora look-alike was gone.

I guess you could say I got into a bachelor-god routine. Every day, I walked the dog, made the rounds of my kingdom, and swam a few laps in the pool. Evenings, I ordered dinner from Underworld Pizza, and kicked back in my La-Z-God recliner in front of the tube.

I didn't realize how long I'd stayed away from earth until I met Hermes's bus one day. After he got all his ghosts into Charon's ferry, he handed me a big envelope. Fancy lettering on the front spelled out **LORD HADES**.

"What's this?" I muttered as I opened it. Then I saw this:

*Please come to a book party
to celebrate 25 years
since the publication of Pandora's top-selling*
Girls are from Marble, Guys are from Clay

"Pandora wrote a book?" I said.

"It's a huge bestseller, a timeless classic!" said Hermes. "Where have you been, Hades?"

"Here!" I said. "In the Underworld. Okay, I'm out of the loop. I count on you to bring me the news, which is clearly a big mistake!"

"Calm down, Hades," said Hermes. "So you didn't know that Pandora is a major best-selling author. Big deal. It all started with the classes she taught at the School for Guys and Girls. Some guy told her she should write a book about one of her courses, and she did. It's about how guys and girls can get along better, work together. You know. Mortals eat that stuff up. That's how she got her own TV show."

"So that *was* Pandora I saw!" I exclaimed. "That whole aging thing mortals do is so confusing." I looked down at the invitation. "I think I'll go."

"Go, for sure," said Hermes. "It'll be a blast."

CHAPTER XVIII
WHO IS HE?

"Giddyup, steeds!" I said. They hadn't made the trip to earth for a long time, and they were out of shape. That day, it took them more than five hours to get there. But at last they managed to drag the chariot out of the cave onto earth. I looked around. Everything had changed. Earth was green and beautiful. I drove slowly down the road. It was four times wider than the last time I'd driven over it. I stopped at the spot where the tiny village of Guytown once stood. Now, it was a city — Athens.

I drove through Athens. Swimming laps in the Pool of Memory must have done me good, for even with all the new buildings and roads, I remembered the way to Epi and Pandy's house.

It had changed, too. There were lots of wings jutting off from the main house. And a second story had been added. Lush greenery now surrounded it.

Lots of little guys and girls were playing games in the front yard. They were running and squealing and having a fine time. Older guys and girls were there, too. Then I realized — they were the parents of the little guys and girls.

I sat in my chariot and took in the whole scene. The sky was blue. The sun was warm. The grass was green. The birds were chirping. Earth had become a paradise! Mount Olympus was a paradise, too, of course. But there, all the gods had giant egos. They were always trying to get the best of each other, build the biggest palace, throw the splashiest party. But as far as I could tell, things on earth were harmonious. Some guys and girls were playing games. Others were holding stacks of Pandora's book. Everyone seemed to get along. I wondered: did Pandora's book have anything to do with it?

I parked and made my way up to the house,

walking through throngs of guys and girls. I passed a couple of gods, too. Cupid was there. From the looks of the guys and girls, he'd been zinging plenty of love arrows. Dionysus stood at one table, pouring wine. Hermes stood at another, selling copies of Pandora's book. I wouldn't trust him with a cash box, but it wasn't my problem. Hera was breezing from guest to guest. The goddess of marriage clearly saw Pandora and Epi and their big extended family as her own grand success story.

Now I spotted Pandora. She was sitting on the porch swing beside Epi. He was an immortal and looked the same as he always had. Pandora had aged, though her hair was still as pink as ever. She'd put on a few pounds, but was still a beauty. She caught sight of me and waved.

"Hades?" she called. "Is that really you?"

I hurried up to the porch. "It is," I told her. "Congratulations on your book, Pandora."

She smiled.

"Hades!" said Epi. "It seems like just yesterday Pandy and I were sitting right here, and we told you we were getting married. And now look at all this." He waved a hand at all the guys and girls at the party. There seemed to be thousands of them. Everyone was having a great time.

"Can you believe it?" said Pandora. "Isn't it wonderful?"

"Wonderful!" I said.

And then my eye caught sight of a strange figure. It appeared to be an old, bent-over guy. He wore a faded blue robe and a floppy hat that hid the top part of his face.

"Who is he?" asked Pandora.

"I don't know," said Epi. "I don't think I've ever seen him before."

I stared at the hunched-over guy. Everyone else at this celebration looked happy and kind. But this guy gave off the opposite feeling. I didn't know why — not yet — but I didn't like him. Not at all.

The old guy slowly made his way up onto the porch. He approached Pandora.

"Are you Pandora?" he asked in a trembling voice.

Pandora nodded. "Who are you?" she asked.

"I watch your show every day and I —" said the old guy. Suddenly he seemed to lose his footing. He stumbled and fell to the ground.

Pandora jumped up, alarmed. "Are you all right?" She ran to the old guy.

The old guy moaned. "My ankle!" he cried. "I tripped on a loose board on your porch! I've broken my ankle!"

"Let's get him inside," Epi said. He and Pandora bent down, one on each side of the old guy. Gently they pulled him to his feet. Then, with their arms around him, they helped him into the house.

I ran ahead and opened the door for them. They carried the old guy into the kitchen. I followed to see if I could help. They put him down on the couch.

"Is that better?" Pandora fluffed up a pillow. "Can I prop up your foot?" She tried to slide the pillow under the injured ankle.

"Ow!" the old guy cried. "You're hurting me! You're killing me! I don't need a pillow. I need a bandage! Get your first-aid kit!"

Pandora turned to Epi. "Do we have a first-aid kit?"

Epi shrugged.

"Everybody has a first-aid kit!" cried the old mortal. "Look under your sink! That's where they're kept."

I hurried over to the sink. I opened the cabinet. Sure enough, there was a white box. Red letters on the lid spelled out FIRST-AID KIT. I picked it up. It was surprisingly heavy. I took it over to the couch where Pandora was soothing the old guy. I felt so bad for Pandora, having this happen on the day of her big book party.

"Thanks, Hades," said Epi, taking it from me. "I guess we did have a first-aid kit after all."

"Water!" the old guy shrieked. "I need water!"

"I'll get you some," said Epi. He handed Pandora the first-aid kit and hurried over to the sink.

Pandora fumbled with the latch.

"Hurry!" cried the old mortal. "My ankle! It's swelling something awful!"

"Hades, can you hold the box?" said Pandora.

I held the box. Now Pandora put a finger under the catch and popped it up.

"Open it!" said the old guy. "Go on, sweetheart. Open it!"

Sweetheart?

"No!" I shouted, yanking the box away from Pandora. "No-o-o-o-o-o-o!"

But I'd caught Pandora by surprise. She was holding the lid, and as I yanked, it came off in her hand.

There was a giant *WHOOSH!* and the room filled with thick black smoke. I couldn't see a thing. But I could hear the old guy shrieking: "Yes! At last she's opened it! Pandora's opened the box!"

CHAPTER XIX

WHAT IN THE WORLD??

BLISTERS

SQUARE DANCING IN GYM CLASS

HOMEWORK

DUST BUNNIES   CAVITIES

LOW-SPURTING DRINKING FOUNTAINS

STAGE MOTHERS   THE BLAME GAME   PAPER CUTS

POISON IVY

RAINY CAMPING TRIPS

163

Finally, the smoke cleared. When it did, I was almost sorry, because I saw several little guys and girls crying and scratching themselves. Their moms and dads started arguing about why the kids were crying. Everyone, it seemed, was suddenly mad at someone else.

The old guy was nowhere to be seen.

Pandora was sitting on the couch, looking stunned. "Hades?" she said. "That wasn't a first-aid kit, was it?"

I shook my head. "This time Zeus disguised himself *and* the old box he gave you."

Epi came over and sat down beside Pandora. "What a mess!" he said. "Zeus packed all sort of miseries into that little box."

Pandora took a deep breath. "Well, shall we go see what's happening with the book party?"

Epi, Pandy, and I went back outside. The party wasn't going well. They guys and girls waiting to buy a book were complaining that the line was too long. Dionysus had run out of wine. He was trying to serve grape juice, but the guys and girls didn't want that. Cupid had run out of arrows.

The goddess of marriage, Hera, was sitting on the front steps with her head in her hands.

Pandora went and sat down beside her. "Hera?" she said. "Did you hear the one about the chicken?"

"Tell me," Hera said wearily. "I need cheering up."

Pandora smiled and said, "This guy goes to the park and sees a girl playing checkers with a chicken. They play game after game. Finally the guy walks over to the girl and says, 'Wow! That's amazing!' And the girl looks up at him and says, 'Not really. She hasn't won a game all day.'"

Hera wrinkled her nose. "Why, that's *awful*!" she said, and she burst out laughing.

All the guys and girls standing around started laughing, too. I couldn't help but chuckle a little myself. Partly over how strange it seemed for Pandora to be telling a joke!

"Pandora!" Epi said, laughing. "Where did you ever hear that joke?"

"I don't remember," she said. "It seems I've always known it."

"Hey, you're not talking in question anymore," I pointed out.

"That's true," Pandora shrugged. "The box is open. I guess Zeus's gift of extreme curiosity has worn off."

"Tell another joke, Pandora," said Hera.

"Another one?" said Pandora. She seemed baffled by the idea.

I thought back to the day when Pandora had been changed from a statue into a girl. Thalia, the muse of comedy, had given her the gift of being able to tell a great joke. It looked as if the checkers-playing chicken was it — a great joke.

Suddenly, a bright light flashed, and Zeus, undisguised, appeared on the porch. He was grinning from ear to ear.

"So, Pandora," Zeus said, in his oiliest voice, "you opened that box. Couldn't stand not knowing what was in there, could you?"

What was sticking out of his robe pocket?

"That's not exactly what happened, Zeus," said Pandora. "And you know it!"

"You opened the box," Zeus insisted. He

turned to face me. "Hades! You lost the bet. Now pay up!"

"Hey, Zeus, what's this?" I yanked on the corner of the thing sticking out of his pocket and pulled out a floppy hat. "My ankle!" I said, imitating his old mortal's voice. "Ooooh, my broken ankle!"

"I don't know what you're talking about," Zeus said. He grabbed the hat and tried to stuff it into his pocket, as if that would make us forget. "Trying to weasel out of the bet, no doubt. Well, it won't work. You owe me, Hades. Plus interest!"

"No way," I told him. "Pandora never opened the box. You may have tricked her into *trying* to open it. But I pulled the box away from her. She couldn't help it if she ended up holding the lid."

"That's true," said Epi. "I was there. I saw it."

"Why do you need so much money anyway, Zeus?" asked Pandora. "Money alone has never made anyone happy, not even a god."

"Oh, what would you know about it?" scoffed Zeus. He looked around. "I thought this was a party. Where are the snacks?"

"Over here, dear," said Hera. She took his arm. "I'll show you." And they went off together to the immortals' food table.

Then Epi sighed. "It's awful that the box of miseries was opened," he said. "Life was perfect. Now it will never be the same."

"We had a good run," said Pandora. "We can't complain."

Had someone given her the gift of optimism? It seemed so.

"And you know," Pandora went on, "all this misery has given me an idea for another book."

I had to smile. Was this my gift coming into play? The gift of always being able to make a good living?

"It will be a book that will make guys and girls laugh in times of trouble," Pandora was saying. "A book that will make them smile when they are down. A book they'll want to read over and over and share with friends."

"What kind of book can do all that?" I asked.

"A joke book, Hades," she said. "Have you heard any good ones lately?"

EPILOGUE

There you have it — the Pandora myth, debunked. So don't go blaming all your troubles on the world's first girl. If you want to play the blame game, try pinning the blame on the world's sneakiest god, my little brother, you-know-who.

When I'd finished writing *Keep a Lid on it, Pandora!*, I was raring to send the manuscript off to my publisher. I had a feeling my editor was going to be crazy about this story. It had plenty of action and a likeable, quirky main character, Pandora. But before I sent it off, I proofread it and found all sorts of things that needed fixing. I cleared up some confusing parts. Then I checked my verbs. I had used *said* and *went* way too many times, so I replaced them with nice active verbs like *shouted* and *rushed*. I even went through the manuscript and did a comma check. After the excitement of writing a rip-roaring story, all this nitpicking wasn't much fun. But I've learned that getting the details right is very important to a publisher. And to you, my readers.

When I'd finished all my fixing, I stuffed the manuscript into an envelope and asked the Furies to drop it off at my publisher's office when they went out avenging. My queen, Persephone, was up on earth making the flowers bloom, so I celebrated typing THE END by taking Cerberus out to dinner at Underworld Pizza.

A couple days later, I started trying to figure out which myth to attack next. Zeus had messed with all of them, so I had a wide choice. I took my copy of *The Big Fat Book of Greek Myths* and hiked over to Elysium, where ghosts of very good mortals go. It's always sunny, blue-skied daytime in the big, sweet-smelling apple orchard of Elysium. I picked a nice juicy-looking apple and sat down in the shade of an apple tree. I bit into my apple and began paging through *The Big Fat Book*. I was so absorbed in reading that I never heard footsteps.

"Hey, Hades," someone said.

I looked up.

"Thalia!" I exclaimed. "What are you doing down here in my kingdom? And — is that — my manuscript you're holding?"

"That it is, Hades," said the muse of comedy. "I've taken a part-time job with your publisher." She plucked an apple off a low branch and sat down beside me in the shade. "They've hired me to read through the manuscripts and make sure there are plenty of laughs."

"And?" I said. "Is there enough funny stuff in what I wrote?"

"Definitely!" Thalia chomped on her apple. "Say, you know what's worse than finding a worm in an apple, Hades?"

"Worse than . . . ?" I frowned. What was she talking about?

"Finding half a worm!" said Thalia, and she doubled over laughing. When she stopped, she added, "I love what you did with my gift to Pandora in the story, Hades. How you strung out that chicken joke until the very end."

"Glad you liked it," I said.

"But tell me, Hades," said Thalia, "what happened to the guys and girls after the lid came off the box that Zeus gave Pandora?"

"They learned to deal with all the problems," I told her. "Bad skin, head lice, poison ivy, bee stings —"

"Speaking of bees," said Thalia. "Do you know how bees get to school?"

"What?" I said, confused.

"They take the buzz!" cried Thalia. "Get it, Hades? Bees? Take the *buzz*?"

"I get it," I mumbled, wondering if it would be rude for me to tell the muse of comedy to buzz off. I could only take so much.

Thalia finally stopped laughing. "Too bad Pandy and Epi never sank that box full of bad stuff in the ocean," she said. "And that reminds me, what lies on the bottom of the ocean and shivers?"

"I give up," I said.

"A nervous wreck!" cried Thalia gleefully.

"I'm thinking of writing about Hercules next," I said, changing the subject. I only hoped she didn't know any Hercules jokes! I handed her *The Big Fat Book*. "Read what it says about him in this book your dad wrote."

HERCULES WAS THE MORTAL SON OF ZEUS. LIKE ZEUS, HE HAD THE COURAGE OF A LION AND THE STRENGTH OF A BULL. HE WAS GIVEN XII LABORS. EACH ONE WOULD HAVE BEEN IMPOSSIBLE FOR A NORMAL MORTAL. BUT HERCULES DID ALL XII ALONE. HERCULES WAS THE GREATEST HERO GREECE HAS EVER KNOWN.

"A hero overcoming obstacles always makes a good story," said Thalia. "Sprinkle in a few jokes, and you'll have something worth reading."

"This isn't about jokes, Thalia," I said.

"No?" Now it was Thalia's turn to look confused.

"I'm trying to tell the truth!" I said. "Zeus makes it sound as if Hercules overcame the obstacles by himself, which isn't how it happened. Hercules was strong. He had great big muscles. But he had an itty-bitty brain. If it hadn't been for me and a certain street-smart lion, Hercules wouldn't have made it past Labor I."

"No kidding," said Thalia. "A muscle-bound mortal, a god, and a lion. Sounds like a buddy story. Hey, have you heard the one about —"

"It's the original buddy story," I said, cutting off whatever buddy joke she was about to tell me. "I'm thinking I'll call it *Get to work, Hercules!*" I got to my feet. "Well, I guess I'd better get to work myself, Thalia."

"Wait, Hades," said Thalia. "One more question. Epi's an immortal, so I know he's still around. But what about Pandora?"

"She lived a long mortal life," I said. "And she had daughters galore. But in time, she came down to live in my kingdom."

"Did she ever get around to writing that joke book? asked Thalia.

"She did," I said. "It's called *The Funniest Jokes in the World*. Pandora asked girls and guys to tell her their favorite jokes. She wrote them down and put the best ones into her book."

"Do mortals like to read joke books?" asked Thalia.

"Do they ever!" I said. "Pandora's book sold millions of copies."

"I never knew joke books were so popular," said Thalia. "Maybe I should write one myself. But I know so-o-o-o many jokes. Where would I start?"

"Pandora's working on a new joke book right now," I told her. "Maybe you could collaborate with her, learn the ropes."

"That's a great idea, Hades," said Thalia. "What's the new book called?"

"*The Funniest Jokes in the Underworld*," I told her. "It's going to be huge with the ghosts."

KING HADES'S
QUICK-AND-EASY GUIDE TO THE MYTHS

Let's face it, mortals. When you read the Greek myths, you sometimes run into long, unpronounceable names like *Hephaestus* and *Prometheus* — names so long that just looking at them can give you a great big headache. Not only that, but sometimes you mortals call us by our Greek names and other times by our Roman names. It can get pretty confusing. But never fear! I'm here to set you straight with my quick-and-easy guide to who's who and what's what in the myths.

Alec (AL-eck) — see **Furies**.

ambrosia (am-BRO-zha) — food that we gods must eat to stay young and good-looking for eternity.

Aphrodite (af-ruh-DIE-tee) — goddess of love and beauty. The Romans call her *Venus*.

Athena (uh-THEE-nuh) — goddess of three w's: wisdom, weaving, and war. The Romans call her *Minerva*.

Athens (ATH-enz) — important city in ancient Greece, sacred to Athena.

Caucasus Mountains (CAW-kuh-ses) — a mountain range between the Black Sea and the Caspian Sea.

Cerberus (SIR-buh-rus) — my fine, III-headed pooch; guard dog of the Underworld.

Chaos (KAY-oss) — the disordered state of unformed matter believed by ancient Greeks to have existed before order came to the universe.

Charon (CARE-un) — river-taxi driver; ferries the living and the dead across the River Styx.

Cupid (KYOO-pid) — what the Romans call the little god of love; we Greeks prefer *Eros*.

Cyclopes (SIGH-klo-peez) — one-eyed giants; Lightninger, Shiner, and Thunderer are three of them; children of Gaia and Uranus, and uncles to us gods.

Delphi (DELL-fie) — an oracle in Greece on the southern slope of Mount Parnassus where a sibyl is said to predict the future.

Demeter (duh-MEE-ter) — my sister, goddess of agriculture and total gardening nut. The Romans call her *Ceres*.

Dionysus (die-uh-NI-sus) — son of Zeus and a mortal princess, Semele; god of wine. The Romans call him *Bacchus*.

Epimetheus (ep-uh-ME-thee-us) — Titan whose name means "afterthought"; brother of Prometheus.

Furies (FYOOR-eez) — three winged immortals with red eyes and serpents for hair who pursue and punish wrongdoers, especially those who insult their mothers; their full names are *Tisiphone* (tih-ZIH-fuh-nee), *Megaera* (MEH-guh-ra), and *Alecto* (ah-LEK-toe), but around my palace, they're known as Tisi, Meg, and Alec.

Gaia (GUY-uh) — Mother Earth, the beginning of all life; married to Uranus, Sky Daddy; gave birth to the Titans, Cyclopes, and the Hundred-Handed Ones; she's my Granny Gaia; don't upset her, unless you're up for an earthquake. The Romans call her *Tellus*.

Harpy (HAR-pea) — one of a flock of horrible, smelly monsters with the head and upper body of a woman and a bird's wings, tail, and clawed feet.

Hades (HEY-deez) — Ruler of the Underworld, Lord of the Dead, King Hades, that's me. I'm also god of wealth, owner of all the gold, silver, and precious jewels in the earth. The Romans call me *Pluto*.

Hephaestus (huh-FESS-tus) — lame son of Zeus and Hera, husband of Aphrodite, god of fire and metalworking; carved Pandora out of marble. The Romans call him *Vulcan*.

Hera (HERE-uh) — my sister, Queen of the Olympians, goddess of marriage; the Romans call her *Juno*. I call her "The Boss."

Hermes (HER-meez) — Zeus's messenger; also god of business executives, inventors, and thieves; escorts dead mortals down to the Underworld. The Romans call him *Mercury*.

Hestia (HESS-tea-uh) — my sister, goddess of the hearth, likes to hang around at home. The Romans call her *Vesta*.

Hundred-Handed Ones (HUHN-druhd HAN-did WUNZ) — three oddball brothers (Fingers, Highfive, and Lefty) each with fifty heads and one-hundred hands. They are brothers to the Cyclopes and the Titans.

Hyperion (hi-PEER-ee-un) — a way-cool Titan dude, once in charge of the sun and all the light in the universe. Now retired, he owns a cattle ranch in the Underworld.

Hypnos (HIP-nos) — god of sleep; brother of Thanatos (the god of death); son of Nyx, or night. Shhh! He's napping.

immortal (i-MOR-tuhl) — a being, such as a god or possibly a monster, who will never die, like me.

Meg (MEG) — see **Furies**.

Metis (MAY-tis) — a Titan; Zeus's first wife.

mortal (MOR-tuhl) — a being who one day must die. I hate to be the one to break this to you, but *you* are a mortal.

Mount Olympus (oh-LIM-pess) — the highest mountain in Greece; home to all the major gods, except for my brother Po and me.

nectar (NECK-ter) — what we gods like to drink; to make us look good and feel godly.

oracle (OR-uh-kull) — a sacred place where a sibyl is said to foretell the future; sibyls and their prophecies are sometimes called oracles.

Pandora (pan-DOR-uh) — the world's first girl; often said to have brought all evils into the world — but we know better.

Poseidon (po-SIGH-den) — my bro Po; god of the seas, rivers, lakes, and earthquakes; one of the XII Power Olympians. The Romans call him *Neptune*.

Prometheus (pruh-ME-thee-us) — the wisest of the Titans, his name means "foresight," as he has the ability to see into the future; known as the creator of the guys.

Rhea (REE-uh) — a Titaness; my mom; wife of Cronus and mother of all the Olympians.

Roman numerals (ROH-muhn NOO-mur-uhlz) — what the ancients used instead of counting on their fingers.

I	1	XI	11	XXX	30
II	2	XII	12	XL	40
III	3	XIII	13	L	50
IV	4	XIV	14	LX	60
V	5	XV	15	LXX	70
VI	6	XVI	16	LXXX	80
VII	7	XVII	17	XC	90
VIII	8	XVIII	18	C	100
IX	9	XIX	19	D	500
X	10	XX	20	M	1000

sibyl (SIB-ul) — a mortal woman said to be able to foretell the future; a prophetess.

Styx (STICKS) — the main river of the Underworld across which Charon ferries the ghosts of dead mortals; oaths sworn on its waters are considered unbreakable.

Thalia (THA-lee-uh) — daughter of Zeus and muse of comedy.

Tisi (TIZ-ee) — see **Furies**.

Titan (TIGHT-un) — any of the twelve giant children of Gaia and Uranus.

Underworld (UHN-dur-wurld) — my very own kingdom, where the ghosts of dead mortals come to spend eternity.

Uranus (YOOR-uh-ness) – my grandpa, a.k.a. Sky Daddy, first Ruler of the Universe, father of the Titans, Cyclopes, and Hundred-Handed Ones.

Zephyr (ZEF-ur) — the West Wind.

Zeus (ZOOSE) —rhymes with *goose*, which pretty much says it all; my little brother, a major myth-o-maniac and a cheater, who managed to set himself up as Ruler of the Universe. The Romans call him *Jupiter*.

THE BIG FAT BOOK
OF GREEK MYTHS

According to Greek mythology, the first mortal woman, Pandora, was created on Zeus's orders as a punishment for mankind. But the story of Pandora actually started long before she was even created. It began when Prometheus, a Titan, stole fire from the gods and gave it to mankind.

Zeus, king of the gods, carefully guarded his secrets, and he was furious with Prometheus. He punished Prometheus by chaining him to a rock for eternity. Every day an eagle ripped out his liver and ate it, and each night it grew back.

Zeus decided to get revenge on man in a different way: he ordered Hephaestus, the god of craftmanship, to create Pandora, meaning "all-gifted." Hephaestus molded Pandora from earth and water, and each of the gods gave her different gifts: beauty, grace, manual dexterity, foolishness, idleness, boldness, cunning, charm, and curiosity.

Pandora was also given a mysterious *pithos*, a large jar or urn. The gods told her to never, under any circumstances, open it. The jar, often called "Pandora's box," contained other "gifts" from Zeus. These gifts were all the evils of mankind: sickness, pain, despair, hunger, hardship, and more. But the jar also contained hope.

Then Hermes took Pandora down from Mount Olympus to earth. He gave her to Epimetheus, the brother of Prometheus and creator of mankind, as a gift. Prometheus had warned his brother to never accept a gift from Zeus. But Epimetheus fell deeply in love with Pandora and forgot his brother's advice.

Pandora, who was extremely curious thanks to her gifts from the gods, opened the jar. Before this time, there were no evils in the world, and mankind lived in peace. But when Pandora opened the *pithos*, she released all the evils that had been trapped inside into the world. When Pandora finally managed to close the lid again, only hope remained inside.

KATE McMULLAN is the author of the chapter book series Dragon Slayers' Academy, as well as easy readers featuring Fluffy, the Classroom Guinea Pig. She and her illustrator husband, Jim McMullan, have created several award-winning picture books, including *I STINK!*, *I'M DIRTY!*, and *I'M BIG!* Her latest work is *SCHOOL! Adventures at Harvey N. Trouble Elementary* in collaboration with the famed *New Yorker* cartoonist George Booth. Kate and Jim live in Sag Harbor, NY, with two bulldogs and a mews named George.

GLOSSARY

chaos (KAY-oss) — total confusion

chariot (CHA-ree-uht) — a small vehicle pulled by a horse

crude (KROOD) — rough and poorly made

curiosity (kyur-ee-AHSS-i-tee) — a desire to know something

ferry (FER-ee) — a boat or ship that regularly carries people across a stretch of water

galore (guh-LOR) — in large numbers

hearth (HARTH) — the area in front of a fireplace

lieutenant (loo-TEN-uhnt) — an officer of low rank in the armed forces

lush (LUHSH) — growing thickly and healthily

optimism (OP-tuh-miz-uhm) — believing that things will turn out successfully or for the best

parchment (PARCH-muhnt) — heavy, paper-like material made from the skin of sheep or goats and used for writing on

scheme (SKEEM) — a plot or plan for doing something

DISCUSS!

I. Zeus was furious with Prometheus for stealing fire for the guys. Talk about the different sides of this argument. Who do you think was right, Zeus or Prometheus?

II. Imagine you were Pandora. Do you think you would have been able to resist opening the mysterious box? Why or why not?

III. Zeus tried every trick in the book to get Pandora to open that box. Why was he so determined to make her open it? What do you think he thought was inside?

WRITE!

I. Zeus gave Pandora the gift of curiosity.
Write about a time you were really curious.
What happened?

II. The box Zeus gave Pandora contained all
the bad stuff in the world. Imagine you
are doing the opposite. Make a list of good
things you would put in the box.

III. All of the the gods gave Pandora different
gifts when she was created. Write a few
paragraphs describing what gift you would
have given her and why.

MYTH•O•MANIA

I

II

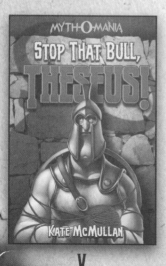

V

VI